# Trainers V. Tiaras

Coming soon by Grace Dent

*Slinging the Bling*
*Too Cool for School*

# Trainers V. Tiaras

## Grace Dent

Hodder
Children's
Books

A division of Hachette Children's Books

ISBN-13: 978 0 340 93217 9

Typeset in New Baskerville by Avon DataSet Ltd,
Bidford-on-Avon, Warwickshire

Printed in the UK by CPI Bookmarque, Croydon, CR0 4TD

The paper and board used in this paperback by Hodder Children's Books
are natural recyclable products made from wood grown in
sustainable forests. The manufacturing processes conform to the
environmental regulations of the country of origin.

Hodder Children's Books
A division of Hachette Children's Books
338 Euston Road, London NW1 3BH
An Hachette Livre UK company

*For Geno – who was a great help.*

This diary belongs to:

Shiraz Bailey Wood

Address:     34, Thundersley Road,
             Goodmayes,
             Essex,
             IG5 2XS

## TUESDAY 25TH DECEMBER – CHRISTMAS DAY

So much for ramming the word iPod into every sentence since last June.

Nan got me a diary for Christmas! A pink leather one with a proper lock and everything. Nan reckons I should 'write down all my secret hopes and wishes' then hide it in a place where no one will ever find it. She never said why.

I would have asked why but she chucked me it, sank almost half a pint of coffee liqueur, then passed out snoring. She was making a noise like when Mum accidently hoovers our dog.

Well, it's Christmas Day and I've nothing else to do, so here goes . . .

### THE SECRET HOPES AND DREAMS OF SHIRAZ BAILEY WOOD AGED 15

- I hope my boobs grow bigger soon and get proper pointy nipples.
- I hope my mum, Mrs Diane Wood, notices the boob growth and stops muttering to my dad, Mr Brian Wood, about taking me to get 'my bits checked out by Dr Gupta'.

- I hope I get a boyfriend this year as there is a running joke amongst my sister, Cava-Sue Wood, and my brother, Murphy Wood, that I am a lezbitarian.

    (Oh and Murphy, if you're reading this, BOG OFF you smelly turd. These are my <u>secret hopes</u>. AND I KNOW IT WAS YOU WHO WROTE 'SHIRAZ BAILEY WOOD FANGITA-EATER' ON THE FRONT OF MY GEOGRAPHY COURSEWORK.)

- I hope I can learn this year how to be nicer to lads in general. I wish I could be a good listener like my best friend, Carrie Draper. I wish I could learn how to flutter my eyelashes and remember funny lines from *Dog the Bounty Hunter* that make boys laugh. I wish I could stop giving boys dead arms and wedgies when they do stuff like fart near me.

- I hope by January, Mr Bamblebury, our headmaster, has forgotten about my part in the Mayflower Academy Winter Festival which resulted in a request for police presence.

- I hope the local newspaper, the *Ilford Bugle*, forgets that our school, Mayflower Academy (formerly known as Marlowe Comprehensive) came bottom of EVERY exam results and behaviour table in Essex. I really hope they stop calling us 'Superchav Academy' soon 'cos now everyone in Essex calls us it and it's totally embarrassing.

    WE ARE NOT CHAVS, RIGHT?

    OK, we're not ALL chavs. Me and Carrie AREN'T

anyway. Uma Brunton-Fletcher down the road is a bit.

- I hope my big sister, Cava-Sue Wood, gets over her whiny-ass self and stops whingeing in the top bunk bed about getting a lemon dressing gown and a pink velour tracksuit off 'Santa' this morning. Does she think I'm happy with my Niko trainers off Walthamstow market? Nobody wears Niko trainers at Mayflower. NOT EVEN THE ASYLUM SEEKERS. I'll have to fake another mugging.

- I hope my best mate Carrie hasn't got an iPod off 'Santa'. What is the point in spending all December drawing arrows all over the Argos catalogue if NO ONE TAKES NO NOTICE?? It is so annoy— oh, gotta go now . . . Mum has made something totally minging with tinned ham in jelly and we're all being forced to eat some.

## WEDNESDAY 26TH DECEMBER – BOXING DAY

Carrie got an iPod. A black one. A 80gb one that plays movies. It's got a message engraved on the silver bit on the back that says: 'For our special girl Carrie at Christmas from Mum and Dad XXX'.

AND she got a silver teardrop necklace from Tiffany. And a Calvin Klein bra. And a New Look voucher for £50. I'm not jealous or nothing. No way. I'm happy for her.

I told my mum. She was on the sofa feeding Penny,

our Staffordshire Bull Terrier, chocolate coins and watching a Jeremy Kyle Christmas special called *Ho! Ho! Ho! Get Out of My Home!*. (It didn't feel very Christmassy.)

Mum tutted. Mum said, 'Them Drapers have more money than sense.' Mum said, 'That girl will be ruined! Ruined! You mark my words! You reap what you sow! She'll turn on 'em, spoiling her like that all the time!'

Mum didn't explain how Carrie 'will turn on 'em', but I reckon she was hinting that Carrie might become a psycho axe-killer or something. Can't see it myself, Carrie is a right softie. Carrie once gave a homeless outside McDonald's in Ilford her Rolo McFlurry as she thought he was lying down 'cos he was lacking sugar. Carrie didn't notice that he had wee all down his trousers and was carrying a three-litre bottle of White Wizard cider.

I reckon Mum just feels guilty as our presents were a bit crap. OK that's a lie. Mine and Cava-Sue's were a bit crap. Murphy loved his presents. Especially his Zombie Armageddon – Bloodbath II PS2 game. He's been in his room shouting 'Die! Die!' and blasting stuff for two days. Actually, there's another hope for my hope list:

- I really hope Murphy doesn't get into the army when he applies in three years' time, 'cos when I ask him why he wants to join up he says 'cos he wants to invade France and 'stuff it right up 'em'. (And we're friends with France, aren't we?)

11pm – Have just asked Cava-Sue what the point of keeping a diary is. She says it's just like having a blog on

6

your Bebo or Facebook but 'cos you're the only person reading it you actually write the truth, not a load of old crap about having 'da phattest life eva' like everyone does in blogs.

Cava-Sue always knows stuff like this. That's why she's at college.

## THURSDAY 27TH DECEMBER

Carrie came round today with her iPod. I hid the Niko trainers under my bunk, but I showed her my pink hoodie and my new gold hoop earrings. Carrie went a bit red then and admitted that she got gold hoops and a hoodie too as a 'stocking filler'. 'But we'll be like twins though!' Carrie said. ''Cept your earrings are much better! Much chunkier!'

'Yeah – you'll be like twins!' gurgled Murphy. ''Cept Shiraz's got bigger norks on her back and looks like a lezboid!'

I hate Murphy. I always remember the day Mum brought him home from the hospital, making a big racket and smelling of poo. He's never changed.

I told Carrie about the secret diary. Carrie said I should definitely write one as I am good at English (when I try) and I will need it when I'm older to give to the person who is writing my autobiography. Carrie reckons I'm bound to be famous when I'm old 'cos I am totally completely unique and people are always laughing at me.

I told Cava-Sue about my future autobiography and she laughed her head off, so maybe Carrie is right.

Carrie reckoned she's gonna take the Calvin Klein bra back to Debenhams in Ilford this week as her mum got her a 34C and that's way too small. Carrie said her boobs are too big for it and keep spilling out of the sides. Carrie said she needs to get her bra fitted by one of those women who take you in the cubicles and feel them for you. Murphy groaned when she said this, then disappeared to the toilet. I think he must have stomach ache.

Everyone in our house has got the bogtrots at the moment. I think this is 'cos Mum defrosted the Christmas dinner chipolata sausages with Cava-Sue's GHD straighteners.

## FRIDAY 28TH DECEMBER

So I get up at eleven and Mum, Dad and Cava-Sue are all in the living-room in their dressing gowns watching *The World's Wackiest Lawnmower Stunts* on Sky One, eating Quality Street. They're all doing my head in a bit, specially Cava-Sue 'cos she's picking out all the green triangles AS USUAL and leaving the toffee pennies. GREEDY BINT. So I ring Carrie and see if she wants to go out.

So Carrie comes round at about one and we walk to the park sharing Carrie's iPod and singing our heads off to *R&B Diva Sensations*, which I think sounds dead class, but then this old dear comes out her house on Dawson

Drive and says she'll get me an ASBO if I carry on screaming – which I'm not – I'm doing the high bits on 'Feel So High' by Bodyjunkies. So I try and tell her that and tell her she wants to get herself a hearing aid but Carrie tells me to shut up and drags me on.

So we get to the park and by this time we are FREEZING and the caff is shut and there's no one there and even the ducks are on Christmas holiday. So me and Carrie hang about the bandstand for a while, then we went on the kiddies' rocking horses, trying to make them rock really fast while listening to well loud Beyoncé and singing, which is a good laugh. Then the park-keeper turns up in his van and shouts at us that we have to leave the play area 'cos he's enforcing a 'no hoodie' rule and he'll get the police if we don't disperse. So Carrie, who is like the least frightening hoodie ever, bursts into tears and then the park-keeper, who's got a nose like a squashed strawberry, looks well guilty and says, look love he don't make the rules and we can stay in the park if we tuck our hoods in. WHY ARE ALL ADULTS MENTALISTS?

So we walk back home down Dawson Drive and Carrie gets her eye on two lads fixing a Vauxhall Nova on Dawson Drive and makes us watch them for a while, but my bum is getting piles sitting on the cold street sign so I say I'm going back indoors.

So I get back about four and Cava-Sue and Mum are having a total scrap 'cos Cava-Sue wants to see this film called *The Crucible* on BBC2 which she reckons is dead important for her Theatre Studies A-Level and she's shouting that she had it marked on *What's On TV* since over two weeks ago which means she's gotta be able to watch it 'cos THEM'S THE RULES. Then Mum shouts even louder that she's been waiting all day for *Stars on Skates at Christmas* with Dale Winton on ITV2 and it's her house and her telly and HER RULES, END OF. Then Cava-Sue starts to get really narky and says that if she can't watch her film she will hate everyone in the house for ever and DEFINITELY MOVE OUT THIS YEAR AND NOT EVEN LEAVE AN ADDRESS. Then Cava-Sue storms upstairs in a right huff and Mum spreads her legs out on the couch and opens some Pringles for her and the dog, which our dog could totally do without as the vet says she is 'morbidly obese'.

9pm – I had no idea that Cilla from *Coronation Street* was so good on ice-skates. She jumped the big ramp for bonus points and everything.

## SUNDAY 30TH DECEMBER

I am seriously, seriously JACKED OFF today. Mum has totally said no about me going with Carrie to Uma Brunton-Fletcher's New Year's Eve house party. She says no way, over her dead body. It's only over the road at number bloody sixty-seven. I can see it from Murphy's bedroom window if I shove me head out far enough.

I am gutted. I tried telling Mum that everyone in Year

Eleven is going and everyone will think I'm a bloody loser if I don't too. Mum just laughed and told me to go and fetch her violin. Mum doesn't play the violin – this is one of her jokes.

I told her that it's only a small party anyway and there won't be any booze and it will be boring and I'll come back at five past midnight. She just ignored me and turned up *Most Haunted* and pretended to be totally interested in an episode about a haunted pub that she's already seen twice and totally knows already that they don't find a ghost.

'Well what do you think, Dad?' I shouted to my dad, who was as usual NO USE WHATSOEVER and just pretended to do a David Hasselhoff Spot The Difference Puzzle in *Pick Me Up* magazine instead.

Then Mum spoke for him and said, 'Your father thinks the same as me.'

So I said, 'Oh pleeeeeeeeeease! Pleeeeeease let me go!' about ten times in a proper annoying voice.

Then Mum shouted, 'FORGET IT!!! I'm not having my daughter hanging about at a house party with them Brunton-Fletcher kids and god knows who else taking god knows what at fifteen bloody years old! You're 'aving a laugh.'

Then she stormed into the kitchen and came back with my plate of potato UFOs and fishfingers, which she sort of threw at me, and the plate was quite hot too as she'd been warming it under the grill. I totally wish I had a social services caseworker like Uma as I'd show them this diary and get Mum banged up for cruelty. (Ideally before tomorrow night.)

I blame Chantalle Strong in 10C for all of this. Last summer when Uma had a party (or a bashment as Uma was calling it), Chantalle went home at 1am (two hours past curfew), fell through the door with her eyes spinning as big as dinner plates, then grabbed her mother and started cuddling her.

'Cuddling me?!' Chantalle's mum told my mum. 'I thought, right, she's GOTTA be on drugs.'

My mother knows all about Chantalle Strong taking an E. My mother even knows all about where Chantalle got the E from. My mother reckons she knows everything that has ever happened to everyone in Goodmayes EVER. That's why it takes her two hours to pop to the bleeding shop for an *Ilford Bugle* and six eggs. She is on bloody surveillance.

7pm – THIS IS THE ANNOYING THING. What has Chantalle Strong got to do with me? I have never ever taken an E and NEVER EVER WILL. As far as I can see E just makes you dance about like a knob, pulling a weird face with drool in the corners of your mouth and the whites of your eyes showing. Do I need to look more like a minger at parties? I already spend every night out holding Carrie's hoodie while she decides which lad to snog. This is so unfair.

7.05pm – AND ANYWAY, knowing my luck, I'd be the

one who would take a pill and end up in an oxygen bubble getting sung to by Westlife (and I totally hate Westlife).

8pm – Carrie just called. She's not allowed to go to Uma's party either. Carrie says she's going to go with her mum and dad to the New Year's party at Luciano's Italian Restaurant in Romford. I told my mum and she just tutted and said, 'LUCIANO'S? Very nice! Well *bonne chance* to them!'

I could tell from her face that she didn't really mean it. Her mouth was all puckered like Penny's bumhole.

## MONDAY 31ST DECEMBER – NEW YEAR'S EVE

10am – I am STILL not allowed to go to Uma's party. I have tried everything. I have tried ignoring everybody, shouting at them, mumbling to myself like I'm having a mental episode, crying dead loud, and my last attempt was telling Murphy to tell Mum that I am upstairs starving myself to death. (I'm not really. I've got a raspberry Poptart and a box of spready cheese triangles under my pillow, not that anyone cares.)

4.40pm – Mum is trying to suck up to me. Mum says we can 'have our own party' – me, her and Dad. She has bought Dad some lagers and herself a bottle of that Peach Lambrella wine you always see advertised on the sides of buses. *Peach Lambrella: the ultimate party perker-upper!* Mum says she saw it on offer and just liked the name.

4.45pm – I hope to god Mum's past getting knocked

up again or the poor brat would get called Lambrella Wood, even if it was a boy.

5pm – Cava-Sue is going to watch some bands play at Trafalgar Square with Lewis from college. Lewis is a boy who is her friend, but not her boyfriend, so she says, which doesn't explain why she's been covering her spots with makeup and sticking panty-liners to her boobs to fill out her bra since noon. Mum keeps moaning that Cava-Sue's got no business going off to central London, which is eleven miles away, and Cava-Sue shouldn't come running to her when she gets trampled by police horses, blown up by terrorists, then raped on the night-tube home.

Luckily for her, Cava-Sue is eighteen and NOT IN PRISON LIKE ME, so she is still going.

5.30pm – Cava-Sue has just come downstairs dressed for her night out wearing BLACK EYELINER. Mum just nearly choked on a chocolate-covered brazil nut. 'Have you been learning to be a clown at that Theatre Studies A-Level, Cava-Sue!?' Mum laughed, ''cos you're certainly dressed like somefin' from Billy Smart's Circus!'

Mum then moaned about the lovely pink tracksuit she got Cava-Sue for Christmas that's still got the TK Maxx tags on. 'What you gotta wear those tatty jeans for!' she moaned. 'All that cash me and yer father spend on keeping you nice and you look like a bag of crap.'

Cava-Sue has just left, slamming the door so loud the Christmas-tree fairy fell off and startled the dog.

6pm – MURPHY HAS GONE OUT NOW!!! He's gone to Tariq's for a firework display. Tariq's uncles have got loads of fireworks left over from Eid so they're going to let them all off at midnight and have food. I can't believe it. Murphy is thirteen years old. He eats his own snot. He spends all day watching *Police, Camera, Action* reruns and has to be forced by my mother to change his underpants once a fortnight. AND HE'S GOING TO A NEW YEAR'S EVE PARTY AND I'M NOT. I hate him.

6.30pm – The first people have arrived at Uma's. Luther Dinsdale from my class has just been dropped off by his dad. And Kezia Marshall too. I am spiralling into some sort of depression that not even my *Hip Hop Honeyz* CD can lift.

8pm – Mum must feel guilty. She has given me a glass of Peach Lambrella. It tastes of fizzy liquid farts but it blocks out the pain.

8.05pm – Actually this Lambrella stuff is not that bad. If you sip it quickly, it just tastes a bit like Summer Fruits washing-up liquid. There are fifteen people in Uma's garden, smoking, shouting and LAUGHING. I am really annoyed now. Don't worry, Mother – I'll just watch the highlights tomorrow on everyone's Bebo flashboxes, YOU OLD WITCH.

9pm – Chantalle has just texted to say Uma's utility room is full of Year Eleven boys from Stratford Hill Academy drinking bottles of lager and where are me and Carrie?

9.10pm – WHERE AM I?? I am stuck in the living-room with my mum and dad who are a bit pissed and dancing to their *Best of Level 42* album! My mother dances like a football mascot. Her arms and feet go at different speeds.

9.47pm – Oh god. My mum and dad are slow-dancing to a song called 'Careless Whisper'. I have got dead bad hiccups and am going to sneak another glass of Lambrella to my room and phone some people.

10.30pm – Why is Carrie not picking up her phone!!!!? Why!? Why has Chantalle or no one even rang again from Uma's to see where I am? NO ONE CARES ABOUT ME. NO ONE. I WISH I WAS DEAD. I feel a bit sick now. Mum has just been into my bedroom and STOLEN my glass of Peach Lambrella back off me and says I should lie down and drink water as my face looks green.

10.47pm – Dear Diary, I amm stilll notapppy aboout not beeein aloowed to Uma's party 'cos. 'COS . . . I am not a kid. And now I have been put to bed like a bloody kid!!!! WHY DOES EVRYONE TREET ME LIKE A BLOOODY KID AND I AM NOT ONE!! What is wrong with me and why are the bunk beds feeling like they are moving. Oh god I feel totally crap. Oh. Oh god. Oh no

# JANUARY

## TUESDAY 1ST JANUARY - NEW YEAR'S DAY

Nobody in the Wood household is speaking to me. NOBODY. Not Mum. Not Dad (no change there). Not Murphy. (Don't care about him, he can go spin on one.) Not Cava-Sue (especially not Cava-Sue as I vommed all over her bunk bed last night.) Even the dog is pretending to be deaf and refusing to play Fetch the Squeaky Bart Simpson Doll.

'Ugggghhhh, Shiraz!' screamed Cava-Sue, when she got back indoors at 2am. 'This room stinks of chopped carrots now! Oh bleeding hell, I hate living here! Why do you have to be such a selfish little git? Mum says you only had one and half glasses of fake wine too??!'

The only clean duvet cover Cava-Sue could find was her old Barbie one. That annoyed her even more 'cos she thinks she's like a total woman since she started at that bloody college.

3pm – I have a blob of Tippex on my forehead and it won't come off. After I spewed I think I tried to Tippex some stuff out of the diary and then fell asleep and got my face stuck to the page. I have scrubbed and scrubbed but it will not budge.

Murphy laughed so much when he saw, I thought he was going to poo himself.

4pm – Carrie just called to wish us all Happy New Year. I told her that I'd had 'a chilled one' with my mum and dad. Carrie sounded like she had a brilliant time at Luciano's. Carrie drank a glass of real champagne called Pikey Hidesick and there was a Robbie Williams tribute singer and everything.

Carrie said the singer was EXACTLY like Robbie but he was called Keith and he had a double chin and was shorter and couldn't really do the high notes in 'Angels' but he was dead good anyway. It was £50 per person and you got your food and the Pikey Hidesick for that too.

8pm – I told Mum about the restaurant and the singer. Mum is still officially not speaking to me but she couldn't help herself.

'Fifty quid?' she said. 'Fifty QUID? Ha! I remember when Carrie's mother used to earn FIFTY PENCE an hour at Goodmayes Working Men's Club, pulling pints!' Mum shook her head and chucked the dog another Sweet Chilli Pringle. 'She used to turn up in laddered tights! Laddered tights!'

What a weird thing to remember.

## THURSDAY 3RD JANUARY

Went to Ilford Mall with Mum 'cos Nan had bought her a foot spa from Boots which she didn't want. 'When do I get the chance to bleedin' sit down?!' Mum tutted.

I felt like saying 'Every bleedin' night!' but I didn't, 'cos she's just started speaking to me again and it's stuff like this that gets me called 'a gob on a stick'.

Mum wanted the foot spa money refunded to spend on 'Back To School' clothes for Murphy. Apparently Murphy needs new school trousers and a jumper as he's grown almost fifteen centimetres since last summer. Mum is dead proud of Murphy growing. I dunno why. He is turning into a giant. I reckon we should sell him to China and he could be in one of those mobile freak circuses what I saw on the Discovery Channel. Mum keeps telling everyone we meet how big Murphy is and making him stand back to back with her to prove it.

Mum said Murphy didn't have to come shopping. Mum said Murphy was allowed to stay at home 'cos 'shopping isn't men's work'. Murphy laughed like a drain when Mum said this and texted Tariq to bring over his Xbox. We left them in the living-room playing Star Wars Battle Front and making fart noises under their arms with their hands.

We saw Collette Brown, Cava-Sue's ex best friend, coming out of Cheeky's Vertical Tanning Salon and Nail Emporium on the high street. Collette looked totally beautiful, like a footballer's girlfriend or something. Collette's skin was really tanned and her hair was all straight and dyed white-blonde. She had long black boots on and a little fur jacket, and big thick gold hoops that actually looked like proper gold, (not like the ones my mum got me for Christmas that are turning the backs of my ears green).

I felt like a right hound standing beside her in my white Umbro trackie top and Niko trainers. I kept playing with my fringe so my hand covered the Tippex blob.

'Happy New Year, Mrs Wood! All right little Shiz!' Collette said. She was talking into a mobile phone and smoking a fag at the same time. Collette's cool like that.

'All right Collette, lovey!' said my mum, her face lighting up.

Collette chucked her mobile into her white handbag that had a big D&G on the side.

'Cava-Sue all right, Mrs W?!' Collette asked.

'Yeah, well not so bad,' said my mum. 'Still studying.'

'Ooh rather her than me!' said Collette. ''Ere, I just had these done, what you reckon?'

Collette showed us her nails. They were dead long and painted pink with white tips.

'Oooh very posh!' said my mum. I didn't say anything. I can never think of anything to say when Collette is about.

'Freebie, 'cos I work there! I got a full set of French acrylic tips! Meant to be forty-eight pound fifty!' said Collette.

Just then a black BMW pulled up and tooted its horn. There was a big bloke with a skinhead in the front.

''Ere, this is my lift, best go, tell Cava-Sue to call me!' shouted Collette.

'Will do, lovey. Take care of yourself!' said my mum.

Collette jumped in and they drove off, playing dead loud R&B.

'Cava-Sue won't ring her,' I said to Mum. 'Cava-Sue never rings her any more.'

'I know,' said my mother, then she looked quite sad.

We brought home Murphy two jumpers in two different sizes. Murphy tried them both on and he liked the bigger one better.

Mum said, 'I'm taking the one that doesn't fit back to Top Man tomorrow.'

## SATURDAY 5TH JANUARY

4am – Woke up in the night proper worried about going back to Mayflower. I totally KNOW Mr Bamblebury will not have forgotten about the Mayflower Academy Winter Festival incident thingy. Kezia texted me today and said that there is a video getting stuck up on everyone's Bebo flashboxes that proves I was the one that caused all the trouble. Our crap PC has got a virus and won't play Flash so I've not seen it yet. I believe her though.

Why, when I try really really hard not get involved in stuff do I always end up as 'A RINGLEADER'?

10am – Carrie rang, she just saw the movie. Carrie said that it TOTALLY TOTALLY looks like it was me who started all the trouble. Carrie said that you can totally hear me singing the dead rude version of the Christmas carol that Miss Bunt with the moustache had taught us, called 'Jesus Was A Very Special Boy'.

I AM SO GUTTED. I totally never made up those words. Luther did!

Carrie said that on the movie all the Year Nine, Ten and Elevens are in the school hall, and the parents are all there (well mine aren't – Mum couldn't take time off from the bookie's) and we're singing the chorus part which goes: *'Oh how the bells begin to chime! La la la la, it's Christmas time! Oh how our hearts all soar with joy! Jesus was a very special boy! Jesus was a very special boy!'*

But me and Uma and Luther and all the back row weren't singing the right words 'cos Luther made up other rude words weeks ago that made us wet ourselves.

So Carrie said that everyone's singing dead loud and then Sonia Cathcart from 10W's dad who is a Seventh Day Adventist stands up and starts waving his arms like a nutter at Miss Bunt. Carrie said that Uma, Chantalle, her, Luther and everyone else just shuts up singing then and it's only me singing, and I'm going: *'Oh how the bells begin to chime! La la la la, it's Christmas time! Oh how our hearts all soar with joy! Jesus was a batty batty boy! Jesus was a batty batty boooooooooy!'*

So apparently Sonia Cathcart's dad hears me and his face goes dead purple and he starts shouting at Miss Bunt that these kids 'HAVE SATAN WITHIN THEM'. Then he shouts that he KNOWS that his Sonia is going to heaven but we'll all be left to roam the earth on Judgement Day with THE BEAST. So then Luther's dad, who used to be a kick boxer, stands up and tells Sonia Cathcart's dad to shut his bloody mush and stop 'being a God-botherer' and one of them 'religious funnymentalists'. So Sonia's dad calls Luther's dad a 'filthy heathen' so Luther's dad gives him a back hand and Sonia's dad starts doing some weird martial arts moves and Mr Bamblebury, our headmaster, has to split them up.

Then Miss Bunt shouts at Nabila Chaalan's dad to stop filming the fight with his digital camera and Uma Brunton-Fletcher's mother shouts at him, 'Yeah, Abdul, stop filming, you bleedin' paedo, you're always here filming! What do you want a film of this for?!'

Then everyone started really arguing with everyone else and Mr Bamblebury got dead angry and shouted that the Mayflower 2006 Winter Festival was now CANCELLED. Then the Bean twins from Year Nine's mother starts crying 'cos she'd spent all night making Asda tea towels into shepherds' outfits and now 'her kiddies won't even get to behold the baby Jesus or anyfin'!!!!' And at some point the police got called and that's how we ended up on the front of the *Ilford Bugle* getting called 'Superchav Academy' AGAIN.

3pm – Of course, at the end of the day, I do feel partly responsible for all of this.

## SUNDAY 4TH JANUARY

4pm – Carrie and Carrie's mum have just bumped into Miss Bunt with the moustache, our English teacher, in the pizza section of Asda. Carrie said that Miss Bunt says that she is no longer our English teacher. Carrie said Miss Bunt is going back to Adelaide in Australia to retrain as a florist. Carrie asked Miss Bunt if it was the Winter Festival what had done it. Miss Bunt said it was that and the constant nicknames she had to put up with from 'some of the kids'. I feel terrible now. I was the one who started off 'Hairy Bunt'.

11pm – I'm a bit worried about school. I can't sleep. It is not helping that Cava-Sue has been getting mushy phonecalls and texts all night. I asked her who they're from and she said, 'Mind your big sneb, beakgirl'. I know they're from Lewis, 'cos I've been pretending to be asleep but I am not.

11.15pm – Cava-Sue needs to start being nicer to me or when I meet this 'Lewis' I will totally grass her up about the panty-pad boobs she wore on New Year's Eve. Cava-Sue is flatter than me. Cava-Sue's baps make mine look like cantaloupe melons.

## MONDAY 5TH JANUARY

BACK TO SCHOOL!!!!

Mr Bamblebury gathered all of the Year Nines and

Tens into the assembly room today and moaned at us about behaviour. Mr Bamblebury said the whole point of Marlowe Comprehensive School's name being officially changed to the Mayflower Academy last September and being given all that money by the Prime Minister to become a centre of excellence was that WE WERE ALL SUPPOSED TO BE TURNING OVER A NEW LEAF!!

Mr Bamblebury really really shouted when he said 'new leaf' and stared at me and Luther and Chantalle and Carrie.

Mr Bamblebury said that he was tired of the blatant disregard for rules, non-attendance and general tomfoolery. (Tomfoolery! I love that word!! Why are some words so good?) Mr Bamblebury said he was not standing for ANY MORE OF OUR DISRESPECT. Then he said that a number of measures were in place and we'd certainly be noticing them over the coming weeks. I don't know what that meant.

Mr Bamblebury said to begin with he wanted to see Uma Brunton-Fletcher in his office at 10am to talk about the FILTHY language and accusations about him and his pet cat on her Bebo site. Kezia Marshall shouted out that he'd have a job doing that as Uma's mother always takes her out of school during the first two weeks of January to go to the Dominican Republic.

Mr Bamblebury's eyes bulged out of his head then and he made us spend the next fifteen minutes singing gay songs about robins and rainbows from the *Come and*

*Praise* songbook, while he stared out the window mumbling things that sounded like bad swear words.

Miss Bunt has definitely gone for good. Me and Carrie went to English today and Miss Bunt wasn't there. We had a supply teacher from Poland instead who had a small face and a long neck and looked a lot like Jar Jar Binks.

I didn't learn her name as she won't be here very long anyhow, so we all called her Jar Jar, not to her face though, just behind her back, (although I have got quite a loud voice so she might have heard).

## TUESDAY 5TH JANUARY

CARRIE DRAPER IS IN LOVE! With someone she doesn't even know. She told me in Maths. This isn't totally shocking news as Carrie is always falling in love. She was in love with Keith the Robbie Williams tribute bloke last week, but he hasn't returned any emails to her and this is after him personally telling her to check out his myspace and everything.

Anyway, now Carrie likes some lad that lives down Dawson Drive. Carrie said she sees him fixing his Vauxhall Nova with his mate when she is out walking Alexis, her mum's Chihuahua. (Walking! Ha – that stupid fluffy thing just gets carried everywhere.)

Carrie said I must remember him as we saw him when we went on our walk at Christmas. So I said to Carrie was it that guy with the strawberry nose who shouted at us and Carrie said no, don't be sick, that was the park-keeper and he was like forty. Carrie said that the lad she is in love with is totally gorgeous and tall and he's about eighteen and has a silver car with alloy wheels and silver wheel arches. I don't remember him at all but Carrie says she's seen him a few times now about Goodmayes and in Burger King once and he is lush.

Nothing exciting happened at school today. That Jar Jar Binks woman tried to make us look at our GCSE set text, *Jane Eyre* by Charlotte Brönte. The book is about a munter teacher who lives in a castle or something. She tried to make us study a page then answer a question about why we thought the woman was so sad. What is the point? I'm not going to pass GCSE English, no chance.

'Are there any queries?' Jar Jar said after we read through a page together.

'Yeah miss, Sean Burton!' I shouted and pointed at Sean in our English set who dyes his hair blond and has a pink Bebo page and always goes on about his Kylie Minogue *Showgirls* DVD and wears spot concealer. Everyone laughed for ages and we got nothing done.

Jar Jar Binks pulled a sad face. I think she's done well to last two days.

THURSDAY 6TH JANUARY

Carrie dragged me and Alexis for a walk down Dawson Drive to see if we could spot 'The Most Gorgeous Boy In

The World Ever' and his mate. They weren't there. Carrie was dead hacked off as she says TMGBITWE is always there poking his Nova with a spanner most nights and yesterday he even looked up and noticed her!

Carrie said this was just her luck as Alexis the dog had just done a poo five minutes beforehand and Carrie was still carrying the poo in a little plastic bag looking for a bin to dump it in. This is why Carrie totally wanted to see TMGBITWE again tonight I think. Carrie is paranoid that TMGBITWE thinks she always carries about a small plastic bag of dog poo.

Anyway, he wasn't there and neither was his mate or the Vauxhall Nova. I hope something happens soon as I am sick of freezing my arse off on Dawson Drive carrying a dog that looks like something my nan once got me for my birthday to keep my pyjamas in.

## SATURDAY 8TH JANUARY

No school today, thank God. Me and Carrie went to Ilford Mall 'cos Carrie needed to take back the too-small Calvin Klein bra. All the usual Year Ten faces were down the mall. Chantalle, Luther, Kezia and like twenty other randoms were all on the third floor hanging about the food court stressing out the security guards by wearing their hoodies up and laughing too loudly and asking the staff at Magic Spuds for beakers of free tap water.

So we were all laughing our heads off 'cos Luther had

just tried to run down the up escalator, when the big scary Chinese security guard who looks like a Triad arrived and said we were taking up the tables where the real people could be sitting so we all had to go. So Kezia started getting all up in his face like a rudegirl going, 'Like what am I bro? NOT A REAL PERSON?' And the security guard just laughed at her 'cos he was like eighteen stone and six foot tall and looked like he could kill her with one flick.

Then Kezia said, 'I got like civil liberties, y'know bredren!'

And the security guard laughed and said, 'You go have your civil liberties outside McDonald's, not in my mall then.' Then he chucked us all out.

Then me and Carrie left everyone and went to Superdrug to look at the nail varnishes. We were coming out of Superdrug and Carrie saw this dead fit lad with tiny cornrow dreads and wide shoulders called Lee Coatchford, who everyone calls Cotch, who used to work for Carrie's dad as an apprentice at Draper Hydration after he got asked to leave Mayflower last year. But then Cotch left Draper Hydration 'cos he said he was going to go in the marines, but then he didn't do that either so it seems.

Anyway Carrie sees him and she says, 'All right Cotch!'

And Cotch sees Carrie and he looked well happy and he's like, 'All right darling, how's it going?'

And Carrie goes, 'Aw not bad, Cotch, just shopping!'

Then she puts her head to the side and made her voice all softer and said, ''Ere Cotch, how's your mum doing?'

So Cotch starts telling Carrie all about his mum who's had some kind of blood cancer thingy and Carrie's saying all the right things back like, 'Well, Cotch, it sounds like the doctors know what they're doing,' and ''Ere, well tell her that me and my mum and dad are all thinking of her.'

After about five minutes, Cotch walked off saying he was dead happy to have bumped into Carrie and he'll MSN her or comment her Bebo pics. Then Carrie puts her arm through mine and dragged me to H&M to look at the earrings, and as we walked to H&M I was thinking to myself, why can't I do that with boys? Why can I never think of the right thing to say?

## SUNDAY 9TH JANUARY

Nan came over for Sunday dinner today. We had chicken and roast potatoes and carrots and Brussels sprouts and peas and gravy, which was nice 'cos Nan cooked most of it. When I woke up at 10am I could smell the chicken cooking and hear my mum giving my dad earache to take the bin bag out and Cava-Sue singing in the shower and Murphy throwing squeezie Bart Simpson down the hallway for Penny and I don't know why that made me feel happy but it did.

When no one was listening, I told Nan that I was

writing in the diary but it was A SECRET.

Nan says that my secret is safe with her and that she is glad as I was always good at writing when I was little and had a good imagination too. Nan said she always remembers how once when I was little I locked Murphy in the under-the-stairs cupboard and told everyone he had run away with some pikeys in long capes and long flappy shoes in a big yellow car with a loud horn.

Nan says everyone laughed their bleeding heads off 'cos they could totally hear Murphy crying and when they opened the cupboard and all looked inside he screamed the house down even more. Nan says that I told everyone that the pikeys must have changed their minds and put Murphy in the cupboard instead. Nan says I've always been 'sharp as a tack'. I'm not sure how this story proves that 'cos I've heard it like a hundred times now and I still think it makes me sound like someone who ends up in the Pupil Referral Unit.

Me and Cava-Sue washed up then and listened to Dave Pearce dance anthems in our room like we always do on Sunday. It's not as much fun now 'cos Cava-Sue reckons she doesn't know any of the songs any more as they're all 'commercial' and that. Cava-Sue doesn't want to sing along with me any more and she definitely doesn't want do any 'hands in the air' bits.

Cava-Sue said she'd rather listen to bands that no one has heard of 'cos it makes it more special. It's dead weird 'cos the more clever stuff Cava-Sue learns at college, the more thick things she says. Who wants to listen to a band that no one has heard of?

## MONDAY 10TH JANUARY

BIG GOSSIP TODAY. Latoya Bell says that Kezia Marshall thinks she's PREGNANT! Latoya says Kezia was crying in the nurse's office this afternoon when Latoya went in to get a Nurofen signed out for period pain. Latoya, who is a right gobby cow, says she saw Kezia in the nurse's 'advice' armchair and the nurse with the calendar out, counting days. I don't know how this proves Kezia is having a baby but it seems to be enough for Latoya, who is telling everyone in Mayflower and saying Kezia is a slut. Latoya Bell said to me in the lunch queue that at Uma's New Year Party she saw Luther going into the utility room with Kezia then shutting the door and coming out laughing.

Latoya thinks I am her friend but I'm not. I just pretend to be 'cos I saw what she did to Chenai Green when Chenai and Latoya stopped being friends. All that stuff with the fake Bebo and the text messages. That was nasty. It's easier to just be a faker. But I ain't going to crawl up her arse or nothing. I ain't no beg friend.

Luther said it was all crap when Carrie told him the rumour in lunch. But then he gave me his cheese and chips 'cos he couldn't eat them and didn't say much else today at all. I hope it isn't true. He wouldn't be a very good baby-daddy. He can't even remember to bring a pen most days, let alone buy nappies and stuff.

## WEDNESDAY 13TH JANUARY

Jar Jar Binks has gone! This other woman turned up instead, who was tall and not fat but quite big. She was dressed in a black jacket and black skirt with high heels, and she had black glossy skin, lipgloss on her lips and a stern voice. She kicked open the door to the English room, then walked in carrying a box of books.

'Year Ten, Stream Two?' she said.

'Yeah,' we all said.

''Ere, are you the new supply?' I shouted.

The woman ignored me. She had those black-rimmed trendy glasses on that pretentious people from the middle of London wear.

'Sit down, all of you right now and turn off your mobile phones,' she said, standing behind the front desk.

We all just ignored her. Teachers always say this but they can't take our property, 'cos that's like theft, we know our rights. The woman leaned forward and stuck both hands down on her desk and stared at us all.

'Get out your mobile phones right now,' she said sort of calmly but dead loudly. 'Put them where I can see them, then turn them all off NOW.'

There was something about the way she said 'NOW' that made me think it would be less earache to just do it.

So I did. Chantalle did it too. Then Luther. Then everyone else.

'Are you the supply?' I shouted again. She just ignored me again.

'My name is Ms Bracket,' she said, then she grabbed the chalk and wrote it in capital letters on the board, *B.R.A.C.K.E.T.*

Bracket!? Like something that keeps shelves up! What does Bracket rhyme with? Spracket!? Hacket? Cack hat? Not funny. I tried to think of a really rude nickname for her but I couldn't.

'I shall be your English teacher from now until the GCSE exams,' the woman said.

No one said anything, not even Chantalle.

'Fabulous shoes,' whispered Sean Burton.

Ms Bracket looked at Sean, then she nodded and said, 'Thank you.

'Right – get out your *Jane Eyre*s,' said Ms Bracket, 'I want to see *Jane Eyre* by Charlotte Bronte on the desk opened at page fifty. If you haven't got your *Jane Eyre*, I've got thirty copies here to borrow for the lesson. Take one, write your name there, and do it quickly.'

We all took a copy. But it was only 'cos it was her first day and we felt sorry for her. And Kezia has been quiet ever since she heard what Latoya has been saying anyhow. And Luther was off today. And Uma was in Dominican. And Carrie likes *Jane Eyre* anyhow as she says it's dead romantic. So that's why we read a bit and didn't make Ms

Bracket cry by throwing stuff at her. She won't last long though 'cos teachers never do.

## FRIDAY 14TH JANUARY

9pm – Carrie has just rang me in a right state. She has just bumped into The Most Gorgeous Boy In The World Ever. Like ACTUALLY bumped into him. She rang me from the toilets in the The Spirit of Siam Chinese restaurant making a weird squealing sound, like Penny our dog does when we lock her in the living-room and try and eat chips in the kitchen without her.

Carrie and her dad Barney were in the Chinese having some food (which is what her and her dad always do of a Friday, her mum Maria goes to spinning class and Barney and Carrie go and eat something somewhere). So Carrie was getting up to go to the loo, the door opens, and it was HIM! Gorgeous bloke. Coming in with his mate to pick up a takeaway. Carrie says he had black Adidas trackie bottoms on and a black jacket and a yellow baseball cap. Carrie says he is lovely and tall and quite thin with a bit of a big nose and he SMILED AT HER as he was walking out. Oh and he is called BEZZIE. His mate was with him and he shouted 'Come on, Bezzie' when their sweet and sour chicken half rice half chips was ready. Carrie said he looked totally lush.

10pm – BEZZIE??! God, I hope that's not his real name. That's worse than mine.

10.30pm – Carrie just rang back and said now she thinks he maybe wasn't smiling, he maybe just had a bit of fortune cookie stuck in his teeth and happened to be looking her way.

## TUESDAY 29TH JANUARY

School was crap today. I hate it. HATE IT!!! I am sick of people telling me what to do all the time. That Mrs Radowitz can spin on one, going on and on in RE about the GCSE exams. They're not until next year!!!! Who cares? I can't wait until next year when I can leave and get a job at JD Sports or somewhere and earn some proper money and NO ONE can tell me what to do EVER AGAIN.

The only interesting bit in the whole day was in English. That Bracket woman is still here doing everyone's heads in making us read *Jane Eyre*, which is sort of funny really as she is proper serious and gets really mad if we even try to talk to each other. So we're all sitting reading this bit about a storm which is meant to be 'symbolic' when suddenly Latoya Bell walks past the English room window and she puts her face up against the glass and she shouts 'Hooooochie slut' and points right at Kezia Marshall.

So we all look at Latoya and then we all look at Kezia and Kezia's white freckly face goes totally red, which matches her hair, and she stands up and she runs right out of the classroom and next thing we know she is outside the class window in the yard right up in Latoya's face shouting well loud. And Latoya tries to say something back, then Kezia PUSHES LATOYA PROPER HARD WITH BOTH HANDS!!! And Latoya falls over and Kezia grabs her by the hair and starts dragging her backwards through the yard and Latoya's skirt comes up past her thighs and I don't know if she was wearing a thong.

Then next thing I saw was Ms Bracket in the yard with them and Mr Stroud too and Ms Bracket is getting in the middle of them both grabbing Kezia and pulling her way backwards and Mr Stroud is shouting 'No contact Ms Bracket! The procedure is no contact!' and Ms Bracket told him to damn well help her or go and call the police. Latoya looked well relieved as Ms Bracket dragged Kezia away.

Kezia has been excluded until next Monday. This is quite bad as Kezia has been excluded once already in Year Ten. It's not her fault. She's nice really, you just don't want to get all up in her face 'cos she's a bit mental. Oh and Kezia is not pregnant by the way. That was just Latoya Bell dissing Kezia 'cos Latoya Bell wants to get with Luther Dinsdale and Luther told Latoya no way at the New Year Party 'cos he thinks she's a backstabber and a fake, which she totally is but, as I say, I'm not getting involved.

Ms Bracket came back into the room after the fight

and she looked really angry 'cos in the fight Kezia had stretched the collar on Ms Bracket's black wool jumper, which looked proper expensive. For the rest of the lesson Ms Bracket just stared out of the window and let us all talk and laugh.

This is what always happens with teachers.

It's the fighting that makes them go.

# FEBRUARY

## FRIDAY 1ST FEBRUARY

School is so crap. I can't wait to leave. I spent loads of this afternoon sitting outside Mr Bamblebury's office with Uma Brunton-Fletcher, waiting for him to get back from his meeting to moan at us about skiving off during the GCSE Geography traffic survey.

I said to myself when I took Geography and ended up sat with Uma that I'd try to stay out of bother. Uma is a proper bad influence on me. I wanted to take Food and Nutrition with Carrie 'cos you get to make swiss rolls and marzipan into *Magic Roundabout* characters but Mrs Brindle can't stand me ever since I blew up her microwave with a can of spaghetti back in Year Eight. That was totally an accident too.

So Mr Gilligan, our Geography teacher, left me, Uma and the rest of our set on the corner of Scalegate Drive at 10.30am and told us to see him back in Room 43 by 12pm with a flow chart of the mid-morning traffic. I thought everyone was going to just skive off, but it turned out everyone else in the group just followed the instructions except for me and Uma, who were rounded up outside Woolworths at 2pm in Ilford Mall by those truancy control weirdos from the council.

God – they are SO crafty. They change the people who work there all the time so you never get to know their faces.

Saying that, we'd probably have missed them if Uma hadn't gone right up – like a proper fool – and hassled the truancy bloke to go in Thresher's and buy her ten Marlboro Lights. The bloke just laughed in her face then flashed his badge and said, 'Bad luck, you're going back to school NOW'. Then another woman who looked like an owl appeared and ordered us to get in the back of her Volvo, which smelled of egg sandwiches, and they drove us back to Mayflower Academy, playing some music on the CD player by a band called The Proclaimers which sounded like two Scottish men straining on the toilet. BRILLIANT.

Mr Bamblebury turned up at 2.30pm. Me and Uma both trudged into his office. He said, 'Nice holiday in the Dominican, Uma?' and Uma just grunted and rolled her eyes at him. Then Mr Bamblebury said, 'So can either of you explain what you were doing wandering about Ilford Shopping Mall when you were supposed to be doing a traffic survey?' So I thought for a bit and this is what came out.

'Well, Mr Bamblebury, what it was,' I said, 'we were actually just on our way BACK through the mall to school when the truancy bods got us. 'Cos we'd been returning a lost cat to a woman.'

'A cat?' said Mr Bamblebury.

'Yeah, a cat,' I said. 'We knew it was lost when we saw it sniffing some bins on Scalegate Drive so we checked its collar and it lived in one of those streets behind the mall. Didn't it, Uma?'

'Yeah, a cat,' said Uma, doing that scary stare at Mr B that she does when she's in trouble, like she doesn't care.

'A ginger one with white paws and a silver collar,' I said. 'And a bell.'

'A bell,' said Mr Bamblebury.

'Yeah, a bell,' I said, wishing I could shut up. 'And a little barrel on the collar with a rolled-up message inside from the owner which said: *Hello, this cat belongs to a little old lady in a house behind Ilford Shopping Mall and this cat is my only friend in the world now that my husband Arthur has passed on and my eyesight is not what it ought to be. So if you find this cat please bring him home to me and I will make you a cup of tea and give you a bit of my homemade shortbread . . .* Then under that she'd written her address.'

'Really? All that on one little scrap of paper?' said Mr Bamblebury. 'She must have had very small handwriting for an old lady with poor eyesight.'

'I thought that myself, Mr Bamblebury,' I said. 'Didn't I say that, Uma?'

'Yeah, she said that,' said Uma.

There was a long silence.

'Good shortbread, was it?' said Mr Bamblebury.

'It was a bit soggy,' I said.

Mr Bamblebury looked at us both, then he drummed

his fingers on his notepad for a bit. For a second I thought he believed me about the cat, even though Uma was totally smirking now so it obviously wasn't true.

Then Mr Bamblebury said, 'Are you two girls ABSOLUTELY DETERMINED to leave this school without a single GCSE between you?'

Uma just sighed. I shook my head.

'Because unless you buck your ideas up you most certainly will. Then you'll be hanging around that mall all day long FOR EVER.'

After he said 'for ever' he left a really long pause.

He made 'for ever' sound well scary, like it was a prison sentence. Uma just shrugged, then I did too, 'cos I didn't want Uma to think I was scared of him even though inside I felt a bit sick. He didn't really moan much though after that. It felt a bit like he'd given up with us.

I wish there had been a cat 'cos I really liked the idea of helping some little old lady who didn't know me, instead of them being scared of my hoodie and crossing the road.

Mr Bamblebury is sending a letter home to my mother. By my reckoning, if he writes it on Monday and Dora his secretary posts it on Tuesday, then I'll need to remember to get up at 6.45am on Wednesday the sixth and put it in the bin.

Letter binned – thank god. Mum was too busy arguing with Cava-Sue this morning to notice. Cava-Sue and Mum used to be dead good friends but they have loads of little arguments these days over what Cava-Sue wears and where she's going. It all started again tonight over a pizza. Cava-Sue didn't want any of her Uncle Franco's Meat Feast frozen pizza or any oven chips either. Cava-Sue said that there are tons of E-numbers in frozen pizza which make her all jittery, so no wonder she can't concentrate at college.

Mum looked quite hurt for about one second, but then she got the hump and shouted at Cava-Sue that it surely didn't take THAT MUCH BLOODY CONCENTRATION TO LEAP AROUND A SPORTS HALL ALL DAY DRESSED IN LEG WARMERS PRETENDING TO BE A SODDING TREE!! Then Cava-Sue looked dead hurt too. Then Mum snapped that *she* ate Uncle Franco's frozen pizza and she managed to concentrate bloody fine all day when she was arguing about racing odds with every wino in William Hill in Goodmayes from dawn to dusk THANK YOU VERY MUCH!!!

Then Cava-Sue shoved her plate away and huffed, 'Well I'm not eating this processed stuff. I'm gonna cook somefin' different, I want somefin' fresh!'

So my mum shouted, 'Help 'yer bleeding self, Jamie

47

Oliver! There's fresh vegetables in the freezer!'

Then Cava-Sue laughed and said that Netto Potato UFOs didn't count and no wonder she was getting fat 'cos she never had any complex carbohydrates. Everyone went dead quiet when Cava-Sue said 'complex carbohydrates'. Then Mum picked up her plate and went into the living-room and ate her pizza on her knee watching *Jeremy Kyle* what she'd taped from that morning about a man who got three women on his street up the duff at the same time.

Murphy ate Cava-Sue's pizza before I could get it. Murphy is not bothered about complex carbohydrates. 'You snooze you lose' – that's his motto at teatime.

There is a crap atmosphere in our house now. I wish Cava-Sue had never signed up for that Theatre Studies A-Level. She is totally up herself these days.

## THURSDAY 7TH FEBRUARY

Went over to Carrie's house tonight. Mum and Cava-Sue are doing my head right in so I texted Carrie and said I was taking Penny for a walk as the fat little pig hasn't walked anywhere since 2006. Carrie was dead happy as she wants us to put our heads together to find us some dates for Valentine's night. I just laughed when she said that as I THOUGHT SHE WAS JOKING. Carrie said they're having a special Valentine's evening at The Spirit of Siam Chinese restaurant and she thinks we should find boys to do a 'double-date'. Carrie is still hoping for some tongue-action with Bezzie with the Vauxhall Nova from Dawson Drive but she's not having much luck with him considering we sat on the street name at the end of his road for two hours on Sunday watching him mend his car and he only looked over twice. I saw his mate though. He was quite nice-looking. He was smaller than Bezzie, with brown hair (not that buff – a bit fat). He looked across once but I just pretended to be texting someone and then he looked again so I yawned at him.

So I get to Carrie's house at about 7pm and the big electric gates with DRAPERVILLE printed on them are locked so I buzz the intercom and smile at the CCTV. I tried to make Penny do all her wees before we went inside, but the annoying fat lump still managed to go and squeeze one out all over the driveway and then run away from me and paddle right into Carrie's mum's koi carp pond with the illuminated statue with no arms. I was giggling to myself 'cos Carrie's house still had a load of the Christmas decorations stuck to the front. If you look closely you can still see the big Santa sitting in the jacuzzi with sunglasses on and the sign which says *HAPPY CHRISTMAS FROM DRAPER HYDRATION!!!* Carrie says her dad's got so much work on right now he hasn't had time to take them down. I think really he's just well proud 'cos his Christmas decorations always get on the front of the *Ilford Bugle* and people drive from as far away as Romford to see them and everything.

So me and Penny went into Carrie's house and we went straight upstairs 'cos Maria, Carrie's mother, was doing yoga in the front room with this quite gay-looking bloke called Bruce wearing Lycra pants, where you could see the shape of his goolies and everything, who's her personal trainer. Carrie's mum Maria is proper lovely. She is ever so pretty and she never shouts and she doesn't look at all like she's thirty-nine. 'You all right Shiz darling?' she said, hanging upside down. 'Give Caz's door a bang, she's been singing her bleeding 'ead off with that iPod on since she got indoors from school!'

I stayed at Carrie's till about 9pm. Carrie showed me the new family photo that her mum has got blown up massive and put in a gold frame for the hallway. It's of Carrie and her mum and dad dressed as cowboys, that they got done when they went to Disneyland Paris. But the photo is printed in a sort of brown colour so it looks like it's one from the olden days. It's well clever. I wish my family did stuff like that. I wish we could all be friends. Last time we went to Fuerteventura Cava-Sue slapped Murphy even before we got on the plane and Mum wanted to go home early 'cos she missed our dog. Maybe it would be different at Disneyland Paris.

Anyway, so then Carrie's mum shouts upstairs that Collette Brown from Cheeky's Salon was coming over to give her a manicure and if we wanted our nails painted we could have them done too. How nice was that!!!? My nails were all bitten though so I said no. I didn't want

Collette Brown seeing my nails with all the bits of skin hanging off 'cos Collette Brown is perfect. I remember when her and Cava-Sue turned sixteen, Collette dyed her hair blonde and got a really amazing tattoo on the bottom of her back that says *Collette* in posh swirly writing. It pokes out of her jeans and she wears her thong over it and it looks so cool. Her and Cava-Sue went out on Collette's sixteenth together and ended up in a nightclub in Gants Hill in a VIP room with some footballers. I will NEVER be as cool as Collette. I wish Cava-Sue still knocked about with her.

So Collette Brown arrived with a pull-along suitcase full of nail stuff. This man dropped her off in an Audi. It was a different one from the one I saw last time. Then Collette did Carrie's mum's nails and then she did Carrie's nails and all the time she was telling us about Valentine's night next week when she's going to a posh place called Oxo Tower in London with this geezer called Vince who runs a firm 'supplying security to businesses', whatever that means. I asked Collette was this Vince him with the BMW or him with the Audi, and Collette laughed and she said neither 'cos Vince had a Benz Jeep. Collette Brown said that she likes being treated like a proper lady by men. She likes getting handbags, champagne, diamonds, that sort of thing off of them. Collette Brown says that if me and Carrie want a Valentine's date we better pull our fingers out of our behinds now and find someone or we'll be in the house together like a pair of lemons. Collette Brown says she doesn't sit in the house waiting to be asked out, she goes out with her mates hunting.

I told Cava-Sue about this later when she was in the bed above reading the *NME* and she said don't take much notice of Collette Brown 'cos she's got a brain the size of a Malteser and she's gone to bed with half the blokes in Romford. This can't be true can it? Collette Brown is dead classy. Her Bebo is so amazing, she goes to tons of well cool parties where footballers from Millwall and Brentford FC hang out.

12pm – God, I really really hope Carrie doesn't find us a Valentine's date. What do you even do on a date? I can't just sit and talk to boys like Carrie can. She'll never find anyone to go out with me anyhow – thank god.

## FRIDAY 8TH FEBRUARY

OH BLOODY CRAPPING HELL. Carrie got a text from Lee 'Cotch' Coatchford last night. Carrie says she is going to ask him if he has a mate and if they want to come out with us on Valentine's night. I said to Carrie stop making us look like a pair desperados and I haven't got any money to go to Spirit of Siam and I'll have to go behind me mother's back and everything! Then I said Carrie's dad won't want her going out with Cotch anyhow 'cos he's got no job or nothing and everyone knows he sells weed. Carrie said, 'Oh stop being negative, Shiraz, do you want us to spend Valentine's night indoors like lezboids or what?' What was I meant to say to that?

I am NOT A LEZBOID at all by the way. I DO NOT fancy girls. Sometimes though I worry that one day I will turn into one 'cos I am just not like Carrie when it comes to boys. Carrie can think about boys ALL DAY LONG. I don't get it. There ain't that much to think about. IS THIS HOW BEING A LEMON STARTS?

## SUNDAY 10TH FEBRUARY

No news from Cotch. Thank god. Went over to Nan's house in Chadwell Heath. We went to Mecca Bingo. There was a special charity night on for cancer where you had to wear a silly wig or deelyboppers and you got a drink with a sparkler. It was well funny 'cos when we got there all the old people were wearing pink afros or big glasses or dracula teeth. Nan borrowed a long black Hallowe'en wig from Casey-Anne, next-door's kiddy. Nan's mate Gill lent me some devil horns. I'm not being funny or nothing but some of Nan's bingo friends are pretty mad-looking anyway so it was hard to tell which teeth and hats were fancy dress.

I LOVE going to bingo with Nan. Nan is the bingo queen. Nan always reckons that she has a bad heart and bad eyesight, but when she gets to bingo she can do six bingo cards at once while smoking a Kensitas Club and talking about everyone else there with Gill. Nan don't even get shaky when they do the live national link up for £40,000!!! I only did one card and my heart was thumping like mad! Nan said if she gets the big national one up she's moving to Spain with Gill and they're going to sit in the sun and drink rum-and-Cokes and find themselves some new fellas, seeing as their old ones have gone and died. Nan said I can come with her and get myself a Spanish fella with brown skin and brown eyes. (Even Nan is obsessed with me getting a lad.) Nan asked how's everything at home with my dad and Murphy and Cava-Sue. I said there's been lots of fights over stuff like pizzas, and yesterday when Cava-Sue bought some stripy tights which my mum hates, and when Cava-Sue taped over Mum's *Jeremy Kyle* with MTV2 without asking which made Mum have a right fit.

Nan was quiet for a bit and then she said well, she don't like frozen pizza either. Nan said that if there's too much noise at my house I can always jump on the bus over to Chadwell Heath and she'll make me some nice chops and mashed spuds. I love my nan more than anything. I hope she never goes to Spain.

It was a right bother getting Nan and her mates home after bingo 'cos Gill won a bingo line and spent the £30 on rum-and-Cokes for her, Nan and their mate Clement. 'There's no pockets in a shroud,' said Gill. They were singing on the bus all the way home. They are worse than us hoodies.

We had English today and that Ms Bracket woman was making us read *Jane Eyre* again. Ms Bracket don't half go on and on about us passing our GCSEs. She is well scary too (without ever shouting). She don't just give up like other teachers. Kezia Marshall said that after she was in that fight with Latoya Bell, Kezia's mum rang the school to complain about Ms Bracket pulling Kezia's arm and giving her post-traumatic shock by shouting at her. Kezia said it was proper weird 'cos by the time Kezia's mother put the phone down from speaking to Ms Bracket it was Kezia's mother APOLOGIZING about Kezia, and that NEVER happens. I don't know how Ms Bracket does it 'cos like I say she never shouts and she don't even use loads of big words or anything.

So anyway Ms Bracket was making us read some pages about the main character, Jane Eyre, who fancies her boss who is this narky bloke called Mr Rochester. In the bit we was reading, Mr Rochester was waffling on to Jane Eyre all about some other woman he fancied who he reckoned was well fit and a right laugh, which was a bit shady of him 'cos as far as I could work out Jane Eyre is quite miserable and has a face like a melted welly.

Ms Bracket made us look at the page for about twenty minutes and think about what was happening. Then she told me to stand up and explain what I thought, and I nearly died 'cos I'd only looked at it once then started doing the *Heat* crossword and sharing a KitKat under the table with Carrie.

'So what is happening in these paragraphs . . . Shiraz Wood?' she said.

'Er . . . well . . . what I reckon,' I said, 'is that this Mr Rochester bloke is being a proper wind-up merchant. I don't reckon he's into that other woman at all. He's just being a player.' Everyone laughed, but Ms Bracket didn't.

'What do you mean, "a player", Shiraz?' she said.

'He's just messing her about 'cos he knows she's into him,' I said. 'He's playing her so she'll be even more keen.'

Ms Bracket looked at me for a bit and smiled. 'I think you might be on to something there,' she said. I couldn't bloody believe it. 'So what do you think she should do then?' said Ms Bracket. Now this sort of stumped me 'cos the first answer was just a wild guess from reading it proper quick.

'Erm, well,' I said, 'I think she should stick in with him 'cos he's got a nice house and plenty of money and that.'

'And is that important?' said Ms Bracket.

'Well, yeah in a way,' I said. 'But specially for Jane Eyre 'cos she ain't got no family or money or nothing and as far as I can see that was like really really bad in the olden days 'cos everyone treats her like a right pikey.'

So Ms Bracket raises her eyebrows at me, then she said, 'So you think a relationship with Mr Rochester, as well as love and security, would bring Jane Eyre more respect from society?'

'Yeah, more respect,' I said. 'Totally.'

'Interesting,' said Ms Bracket. 'That's a really good point, Shiraz, please sit down.'

Ms Bracket smiled at me as I sat down. It felt really weird in my stomach, 'cos none of the teachers smile at me in school and they never ever say 'good point'.

## TUESDAY 12TH FEBRUARY

WHAT A SHAME – still no word back from Cotch about the double-date. Aw, pity. I was SO SO looking forward to that one . . . I AM SAVED! I have worried for the entire week that Carrie was going to set me and her up on some crap date with Cotch and some other random – but it's too late now, she hasn't managed it. Ha ha ha ha ha ha!!!!!

## WEDNESDAY 13TH FEBRUARY

BOLLOCKS

## THURSDAY 14TH FEBRUARY – ST VALENTINE'S DAY

HORRIBLE DAY. Got up at 8am and watched the GMTV Valentine's day special with Cheggers running all over the place with stupid mushy messages for people. (BABY-BOO-BOO I WUV YOU HEAPS – TREVOR XXX)

At breakfast Cava-Sue opened a Valentine's card

from Lewis.

'Ah, so he IS your boyfriend?!' I said. She just pulled a face at me like 'Whatever?' but I could tell she was well happy. Lewis's card weren't up to much. It just looked like a bit of old Coco Pops packet with bits of tinsel and glitter stuck to it. ''Ere, Cava-Sue, did he make that himself?!' I said.

'Yeah, he did actually, he's very creative,' Cava-Sue said and she looked proper chuffed, which was weird 'cos it was like something a five-year-old with learning difficulties would make in playschool, and if he really liked her then surely he'd get her one of them big posh ones from Clinton's Cards that are a metre tall and cost a tenner???

Maybe if she shaved her legs more he might. But I didn't say that, I said, ''Ere, when are we going to meet him then?'

And Cava-Sue just shook her head and said 'Never'.

Then Murphy walks in and said, 'Oi Shiraz, look what I just found on the doormat!' and handed me this envelope which looked like it was a Valentine's card, but it didn't have a stamp on it, so stupidly I rip it open with a half-grin on my face and it was an advert ripped out of the *News Of The World* for the Transform Boob Enlargement Clinic with *Better luck next year NO BAPS!* written on it in Murphy's handwriting. Cava-Sue said that if I ever kill Murphy then she will totally take my side in court so I get a suspended sentence for manslaughter, not done for murder, which was kind of her.

So I get to school and Carrie is standing in the cloakroom looking well excited. Least I think it's Carrie but I have to look twice as her skin looks browner than Nabila Chaalan's 'cos she's done a St Tropez fake tan and dyed bits of the front of her brown fringe blonde. She looked amazing. Carrie is all hyped up about our date with Cotch and his mate Eric and she can't understand why I'm not excited too and haven't even brought a proper change of outfit for the date, which isn't at Spirit of Siam any more but at Burger King drive-through 'cos Cotch has cash-flow issues. So then I got a bit narky with Carrie and said to her, 'What's all the big fuss, Carrie? You don't even fancy Cotch!'

And she said, 'Yeah, OK Shiraz, maybe Cotch isn't Mr Right, 'cos Bezzie from Dawson Drive is, but maybe Cotch is Mr Right Now.' Which didn't make any sense at all whichever way I thought about it.

So anyway, school seems to last for ever, then finally we get to Carrie's house and spend about two hours getting ready. Carrie does my eyeshadow and lipstick, which makes me look like Sideshow Bob, and makes me wear one of her leopard-print hair scrunchies and her diamante dangly earrings in the shape of dolphins which I don't like but Carrie says they go with my pink hoodie and 'bring out my eyes'. Then we go to Burger King and wait for 'our dates' who are meant to turn up at 6.30pm but don't until 7.40pm 'cos they were watching *Pimp My*

*Ride* and dropping round something to someone, which all sounded well shady. By that point I was starving so I had a Whopper meal which I was halfway through eating when they arrived.

My one, Eric, had really pale skin and buggy eyelids and was quite short with a blue Barbour jacket. He smelled like that smoky skunky smell that's always wafting about on the top deck of the bus or round at Uma Brunton-Fletcher's house. I didn't fancy Eric at all. He had really baggy jeans and pants showing (that needed a good boil wash) and his eyes were half shut when he spoke so it was difficult to know whether he was awake or even knew it was Valentine's day or even knew I was there.

About ten minutes after they arrived, Eric finally nodded at Cotch and said, 'Goodskunk, aight?' so I knew he was alive. Then he stared at my chest for about ten minutes, probably trying to work out where my baps are, so I zipped my hoodie right up. Eric never said much after that and when he did I found it dead hard to concentrate as he had this big yellow zit on the side of his head that needed squeezing.

Cotch looked dead gorgeous as usual but well wasted, like he'd had a bottle of Nightnurse for his tea or something. He'd brought Carrie a little teddy which she looked totally ecstatic about, like he'd dived in the sea and fished her out that bloody necklace off the *Titanic* or something. I knew for a fact that Carrie had much better, bigger teddies at home and she was just pretending to be happy and not notice that the teddy looked a bit second-hand and she'd rather be with Bezzie with the Vauxhall Nova. That's the BIG DIFFERENCE between me and Carrie, she is dead good at pretending. Then Cotch asked Carrie to go for a walk by themselves over by PC World, leaving me in Burger King with Eric, who I'd started to realize reminded me of a giant toad.

After about ten minutes of silence, Eric mumbled to me do I want to go and stand behind Allied Carpets and build a spliff with him 'cos the CCTV ain't never switched on round there and I said, 'No, it's going to rain, and I don't smoke weed anyway and I'm going home 'cos I promised my mum I'd clean up the back garden after the dog.' (That was a lie about the dog. I told you I was a bad faker.) So Eric said I should have some spliff 'cos it might chill me down a bit and I said, 'Mate, if it makes me as chilled down as you I'll give it a swerve 'cos you act like you got brain damage.'

Then after about four minutes he realized what I'd said and said, 'Well go spin on one, you moody bint,' and I just laughed and walked off home.

Then Carrie caught up with me by the traffic lights and put her arm round my shoulder and said, 'You all right Shiz?'

And I said, 'Yeah, but that clown was doing my head right in.'

And I thought she would be mad 'cos I spoiled her date with Cotch, but Carrie didn't say anything for about a minute and then she chucked back her head and laughed dead loud and said, 'Yeah they are right pair of clowns, I know. Come on Shizza, let's go home.'

We went back to Carrie's house and she got us both big bowls of Ben & Jerry's with tons of strawberry sauce on them and I sat and ate mine and didn't speak and worried for a long long time that I am a lezboid after all, 'cos if that's what having a boyfriend is like I don't want it ONE LITTLE BIT.

## MONDAY 18TH FEBRUARY

I was in bother quite a lot at school today. I don't know why. Some days I just wind the teachers up all day long. In Geography I got sent out for talking. In Maths, me Uma, Kezia and Carrie got the back row seats and that meant we never did anything but send texts. In Religious Studies we had a class debate about world famine but I'm no good at debating 'cos some people's opinions are so totally stupid that I can't be bothered to listen. Like Sonia Cathcart's. She reckons we should just pray to Jesus Our Saviour and then everything will be OK. How can we stop babies dying every day in Africa? Let's all pray!! And what if babies keep on dying anyhow, Sonia? We should just all pray even harder! Yeah OK Sonia, you bleeding nutjob. So I said this proper loud and got into trouble for being 'prejudicial'. This is just like two weeks ago when we were debating Islam and I said that I wasn't being funny or nothing but Nabila Chaalan's mother looks well unapproachable when she comes down the school gates in her dalek outfit. Yeah, I know I was meant to call it 'the veil' or whatever but Nabila knew what I meant. Sometimes I feel like we live in a world where no one wants to hear the truth. Next week we are doing Judaism. Mrs Radowitz says I should practise saying things through quietly in my head and working out how they sound before I say them out loud 'cos some words can sound 'stigmatizing'. I said I would try.

Then I went to English and realized I'd not brought my *Jane Eyre* or done the homework. Ms Bracket wouldn't even hear my excuse. She stuck me on a Friday lunchtime detention. She is a bleeding nightmare.

## THURSDAY 21ST FEBRUARY

Uma Brunton-Fletcher's brother, Clinton, got out of Young Offenders' today. My mum totally won't let me go to his coming home party even though Uma was showing off all day about all the Peach Lambrella and prawn ring and trifle her mum has bought from Iceland for the buffet. Mum is definitely prejudicial towards the Brunton-Fletchers. The moment I told her that Clinton Brunton-Fletcher wasn't locked up no more she went straight to Mr Patel's pound shop and bought a 'Beware Of The Dog' sign with a picture of a Staffy on it and stuck it in the living-room window. The Staffy on the sign looks nothing like our Penny. For a start it's sitting upright and looks awake and NOT lying on its back with its paws in the air snoring with a belly full of Cheese and Chive Pringles. I pointed this out to Mum and she laughed well loud for ages and said that Penny was having a day off.

11pm – Now I come to think, I don't know whether Clinton is a 'Brunton' or a 'Fletcher' or a 'Brunton-Fletcher'. I don't know who his dad is. I just asked Mum 'cos she knows stuff like this. She reckons last time he was up in court for TWOCing that Merc, he was in the *Ilford Bugle* as 'Brunton-Fletcher', which made her laugh 'cos he don't look like any of them in that house. Mum says Clinton is the spit of a bloke called Swanny who used to sell cheap fags down the Ilford Social Club. 'And all I'm saying,' said Mum, 'is that his mother, Rose, was never short of a packet of Embassy Red, if you know what I mean?'

I pretended to NOT know what she meant. Mum talking about sex makes me want to vomit.

FRIDAY 22ND FEBRUARY

I went to Ms Bracket's detention today. It was less trouble than skiving. Ms Bracket already warned me that if I didn't show that she'd keep tracking me down and making it doubly bad, and the thing is with her that she bloody would. She's a bit nuts I reckon. Sonia Carthcart says that her dad, who is on the parent governor board, says that Ms Bracket was one of Mr Bamblebury's chief weapons to get Mayflower on track. Huh. *BONNE CHANCE* TO HER! So I go in and there's Uma and Latoya and a few other usuals and I sit down and Ms Bracket gives me this exercise where I have to look at the first pages of *Jane Eyre* and find words that the author has used to create 'sympathy' for the lead character. That was well easy, so I just did it 'cos I was hungry and Friday is one of the days they do chips in the lunch hall.

'So, not too phased by that then?' Ms Bracket said, when she saw what I'd written.

'No,' I said.

And she said, 'Why is it not that easy in class?'

'Dunno,' I said.

Then she said quietly so only I could hear, 'I've been doing a bit of investigating about you, Miss Wood,' and I thought: Oh here we go, earache. Then she said, 'It transpires that if your SAT scores are anything to go by, brain-wise you're in the top half of the year.'

I just shrugged at her then and stared ahead.

'And I spoke to Mrs Radowitz and Mr Gilligan today,' she said, 'and they both said the same thing. Bright girl. Probably could do A-Levels. But she couldn't give a damn.'

I just scowled at the silly old bag then, 'cos she was getting on my nerves.

'Always in trouble,' said Ms Bracket, 'always being chucked out of class. Excluded once. Chucking it all down the drain.'

I just zoned out then and tried to do that scary stare Uma does.

'What's the plan then after GCSEs next year, Shiraz?' she kept on moaning. 'Have you thought of staying on at college? You know from next year we'll have a sixth form here too?'

I just stared at her and said nothing. I was going to say that college is full of up-themselves folk doing A-Levels in nothing useful and scrounging off the system, a bit like our Cava-Sue, and I was going to get myself a job in a sports shop or something, but I just shrugged again 'cos I don't have to explain myself to no one and eventually she let me go. SHE IS A NIGHTMARE.

## SUNDAY 24TH FEBRUARY

Carrie has NOT been put off boys by the Cotch/Eric disaster. In fact she's worse than ever. Especially now she's found Bezzie with the Vauxhall Nova's profile on Bebo. What happened was that Carrie was on her iMac the other night and she went on to Cotch's Bebo to leave him a comment 'cos she's been giving him a bit of a swerve since Valentine's and she wanted to know if he wants the teddy back to give to another girl seeing as the date never really happened. So she clicked on one of her mates and then she just kept on clicking their mates and seeing who was there from Ilford and Goodmayes and Romford that we knew. Then after about five minutes of random clicking she said she couldn't believe it but THERE WAS BEZZIE!!! Or BEZZIE KELLEHER as is his full name. Oh and his mate with the brown hair and the fat bum is called WESLEY BARRINGTON BAINS II. (As in Wesley Barrington Bains the Second, like there was a first one and he is the second!!)

And they have a grime collective called the G-Mayes Detonators!!!! Carrie let me hear one of their tracks last night called 'We Got Da Beef' which was basically Bezzie bragging about how brilliant his life was for ten minutes over human beatbox. Carrie thought it was amazing. She has downloaded it on to her iPod and has listened to it fifty-six times since.

I went home quick before the words 'double-date' came up again.

# MARCH

## MONDAY 3RD MARCH

What a crap day. Mr Brightwell from the career advice service came to Mayflower to visit Year Tens this afternoon. We all had to go in and see him one by one and talk to him about what we wanted to do next year after Year Eleven, which ISN'T THAT FAR AWAY so the teachers keep moaning ALL THE TIME.

Mr Brightwell was sitting in one of the IT labs wearing the same green jacket with the leather pàtches on the elbows and the tinted glasses what he used to wear when he did supply teaching at Mayflower, which makes him look like one of them blokes off of ITV's *Britain's Scariest Paedos* or something – even though he isn't a paedo, he's OK. I quite liked Mr Brightwell. He was a totally rubbish supply teacher though. He was always forgetting what class he was meant to be taking, or losing his bag, and eventually he stopped doing supply teaching at Mayflower and Latoya Bell told everyone that her mum said that he'd gone a bit loony 'cos she saw him down the social security doing a claim, but Latoya Bell is a faker and says all sorts to get attention on herself, so that's probably not true.

Anyway, all I know is Mr Brightwell was rubbish as a

supply so I'm not sure how he even has a job himself let alone a job telling everyone else how to get a job, but I didn't say that to his face 'cos I did what Mrs Radowitz said and thought through quietly in my head how that sounded and I reckon it probably was 'prejudicial' and 'stigmatizing' towards folk who just happen to look a bit like paedos but who aren't.

Everyone else in 10W had something worked out to tell Mr Brightwell, aside from me. Carrie reckons she wants to be a nail technician and tanning supervisor like Collette Brown at Cheeky's and Luther Dinsdale wants to start his own grime collective 'cos he's got some pretty good rhymes and his dad knows people who have a recording studio in Stratford and run a pirate called RUDE FM so he reckons he can get a slot. Kezia wants to be a singer 'cos she always does karaoke at Goodmayes Social Club and once won fifty quid of Iceland vouchers and everyone said she should go on *X-Factor*. Uma Brunton-Fletcher wants to be a model 'cos she's dead tall and has the 'right attitude', or so she keeps saying but she's for ever hanging about Oxford Circus Top Shop on Saturdays and it's not like anyone from one of the posh agencies has picked her out to be one or anything, (probably 'cos she has front teeth like a llama).

So I saw Mr Brightwell and he asked if I was thinking of staying in education and I said no and he said, 'What about an NVQ?'

And I said, 'No I want to get a job in JD Sports or

somewhere 'cos I want to earn some proper money.'

So Mr Brightwell said how am I coming on with Maths and English GCSE?

And I said, 'Dunno, ask my teachers.'

And he said, 'Well, it's difficult to get your foot in the door in retail without a Maths and English GCSE, Shiraz.'

So I said, 'Well if I can't get a job in a shop or something I'm going to be on telly as I think I'm quite unique and the stuff I do is proper mad.'

Mr Brightwell sighed quite loudly then and said, 'Like what?'

And I said, 'Well I always say exactly what I think and if I was on a TV show I would definitely cause drama 'cos I say what I think to people's faces.'

So Mr Brightwell said, 'Well that's not enough to make a career out of, Shiraz.'

And I said, 'Well how come Tabitha Tennant from Dagenham who got kicked off *Big Brother* for breaking rules was in the *Sun* last week saying she made two-point-two MILLION QUID last year just from stuff like her new TV show called *Tabitha's Tantrums* on Living TV where they just film her doing stuff like getting her hair done and going around being well gobby.' I said I could TOTALLY do that 'cos if I went on *Big Brother* I'd cause more friction than Tabitha.

Mr Brightwell looked really depressed then and said every girl in Essex wanted to be Tabitha Tennant but that was 'cloud cuckoo land' and we needed to think of a more 'viable option for the future'. He typed all of my strengths and weaknesses into the computer and some of my 'guesstimated' grades for GCSE too and said that he would help me find a work placement to give me a taste of the job world. When I looked at the paper what he'd printed out it said: *Tilak Foods – Unit 57, Bishop Fledding Industrial Estate, Goodmayes.*

Mr Brightwell said it was a small factory that supplies foods like samosas and pakoras and stuff to newsagents and garage chiller cabinets. He said I should write them a letter to see if they can give me a placement. I took the piece of paper and left the IT lab and felt a bit weird.

Mr Brightwell is rubbish. I don't know how he has a job.

## FRIDAY 7TH MARCH

We got to meet Cava-Sue's boyfriend, Lewis, tonight!!! Well, for about fourteen seconds. That's all Cava-Sue would let us see of him and even then she was standing in front of him in the living-room door answering all our questions like he had learning difficulties. He's called Lewis and he is studying Art A-Level, that's all we got to know.

Mum blackmailed Cava-Sue to bring him home 'cos she said she would only lend Cava-Sue a tenner to go out with Lewis if we could all have a butcher's at him. Mum said this Lewis could be a bloody psycho or anything for all that we knew. Mum kept moaning on that when she met Dad in 1985 she brought him home to meet her mother within a fortnight for a cup of tea. 'Didn't I, Brian?' my mum kept saying. 'You came and met my mother and had a cuppa after a fortnight? You remember, Brian?'

My dad made a face like he definitely DID remember. I don't remember Mum's mum at all 'cos she died when I was like three or something but Dad always says that me and Cava-Sue take after her 'cos she called a spade a spade too, whatever that means. Dad says the first time he went round to see his future mother-in-law, the first thing Gran did was look at his hair and pull a face, then open up her handbag and pull out a comb and say, 'I reckon you'll be needing this.'

Lewis ain't much to write home about. The blokes at Cava-Sue's college can't be up to much if this is the best she can do. Lewis is the same height as Cava-Sue (medium height) and wore a white shirt that was like a school shirt with a red T-shirt underneath and tight black jeans and baseball boots.

His hair is quite long on the top and short at the back and I reckon he had black hair dye in his hair. Weirdest of all he was wearing A WHITE TIE. Not one single thing he had on was a proper label like Hackett or Adidas or Nike, it all looked like it was from Save The Children in Ilford. I said this to Cava-Sue when he popped to the loo and Mum was sticking the kettle on, and she told me to shut my trap or she'd tell Mum she saw me in Ilford Mall this afternoon when I was meant to be at school, so I shut right up then.

Cava-Sue has gone to a club near Oxford Street in London called Young and Lost to see a band called DIY Taxidermy. I know this 'cos I was earwigging on her phone call and I found a flyer in her college bag when I was nicking a pen to do my *Heat* crossword. Cava-Sue has LIED to Mum!! She said she was just going to the Wetherspoon's in Goodmayes then to Lewis's house for a bit 'cos she knows Mum don't like her going to central London on nights out.

I agree with Mum, central London is full of all sorts of paedos and terrorists. I don't know why Cava-Sue needs to go there. Maybe she thinks if she goes to clubs in central London she might meet someone a bit better than Lewis 'cos, let's face it, he's never going to keep hold of our Cava-Sue if he keeps turning up in his old school uniform and bringing her 'pieces of his art' made from bits of pasta and ribbon glued to old Poptart boxes. What a freak.

My mother didn't say anything about Lewis when he went. She just shook her head. If you knew her like I do, you'd know that's not good.

3am – Cava-Sue has just got back from central London. I asked her if she had a good time and Cava-Sue said it was probably the best night of her whole life EVER then she took about three goes to climb the bunk bed ladder and fell asleep on top of the duvet with all of her clothes on.

## SATURDAY 8TH MARCH

Went to Ilford with Carrie today and we had a look around Top Shop and Superdrug for a while but it was a bit cold for just hanging on the benches so we went and sat in McDonald's and I got a McChicken Sandwich and a strawberry milkshake and Carrie got a Fillet o' Fish and a Rolo McFlurry and we sat in the window watching all of the folk passing by and we played That's Your Boyfriend, which usually makes us both laugh so much we can hardly breathe. Basically, I point at some lad and go, ''Ere Carrie, that's your boyfriend,' and it's always some geezer with, like, no hair or a big fat bum or yellow teeth.

Then Carrie says ''Ere, Shiraz, well THAT'S your boyfriend,' and when I look it's some forty-year-old bloke with a beard and all his stuff in a tartan shopping trolley.

So then I go, ''Ere Carrie, THAT'S your boyfriend,' and when she looks it'll be some little hundred-year-old Chinese bloke carrying a tray of vegetables back from the market.

We can play this game for hours and usually we never ever get bored of it but today Carrie was a bit down. Carrie said she is completely totally pissed off as she feels like this whole thing with Bezzie Kelleher is just going nowhere. So I said to Carrie, 'What whole thing, you nutter?!'

And she said, 'Exactly.' Then she told me that she invited Bezzie as a friend on her Bebo last week and about four days later he accepted which was fair play 'cos he hadn't logged in since then but when he did accept she left him a comment saying hi but he didn't even comment her back.

I said to Carrie, 'Well maybe he don't check his Bebo that often 'cos I've not checked mine for like four weeks,' ('cos our crap £200 computer has got a virus and Mum won't get it mended 'cos she says we just use it for rubbish anyhow). Carrie just looked sad then and said that Bezzie Kelleher was breaking her heart.

I laughed well loud when she said that but then I felt bad 'cos I realized Carrie meant it.

So we walked back through the town centre to get the 679 bus home and we saw Collette Brown coming out of Cheeky's with a big smile on her face carrying a box, so we stopped to say hello. Collette Brown was well excited and she showed us what was in the box and I couldn't bloody believe it. It was a TIARA. A silver one with diamonds in it like a princess would wear. Collette Brown said it was a pressie from her new boyfriend, Lennox, and she was off to Curl Up and Dye hair salon to get Jez who has won awards for his hairdressing in Essex to put her hair up and weave the tiara in the front.

Collette was going to a ball that night in Epping Forest and the theme was Royals and Rogues, which was going to be amazing 'cos all the girls dress as princesses and the blokes dress as gangsters. Collette said that she'd had her eye on Lennox for ages 'cos he plays poker in the salon after hours with Earl who owns Cheeky's. Collette said the first time she met Lennox she rang him up afterwards and asked him out for dinner herself 'cos 'she who dares wins'. Collette says blokes love it when girls take the lead. Carrie listened to all this and then she was dead quiet all the bus journey home. I asked her what she was up to tonight and she said, 'She who dares wins, Shiraz.' Then she got off.

WHAT IS CARRIE DRAPER UP TO?

## SUNDAY 9TH MARCH

OH BLOODY HELL. Carrie has only gone and sent a bloody message to Bezzie Kelleher's Bebo saying that she really likes his 'sound' and can she come over and meet him!!! And can she bring me too to meet Wesley Barrington Bains II??? Oh god no. Carrie Draper is a proper liberty. Sometimes I wish I kicked about with Sonia Cathcart 'cos at least if I was spending all my time praying to the Baby Jesus it might be better than hanging about Burger King drive-through getting my non-existent baps leered at by a boy who looks like a toad, or going over to bloody Dawson Drive to hear 'Who Got Da Beef?' played live. I hope he doesn't write back. Please Baby Jesus don't let him write back.

## TUESDAY 10TH MARCH

Bezzie has not written back. I always reckoned Bezzie looked a bit up himself. Whenever we sat on the street name near his house when he was fixing his car he always pretended he didn't notice us when I knew full well that he could hear us singing and could DEFINITELY smell our chips. Carrie says she is thinking of going out with Cotch again just to teach Bezzie a lesson. HOW WILL IT TEACH HIM A LESSON?? I never want to be in love if it turns you this mental.

## THURSDAY 13TH MARCH

STILL NO WORD FROM BEZZIE. THANK YOU BABY JESUS!

Homework tonight was to write a letter asking if we could have a work placement. Mr Brightwell said that we've got to think of all the reasons why we'd be a 'positive attribute to the company'. This is well hard. I rang Mr Tilak from Tilak Foods today for more details of the placement and he said basically it would involve counting six packets of pakoras or whatever out of a chute and into a box, then Sellotaping the box and making sure the food items don't jam in the machine. I told Mr Tilak I've got a low GCSE guesstimated grade in Maths, and he just mumbled it doesn't matter as long as I show up on time and don't eat the pakoras. He said I have to put my application in writing.

I asked Mum what I should write and she said, ''Ere, I dunno Shiraz. Tell him you won't pick your nose near the bhajis and you can count to six all by yourself.' Then her, Murphy and Cava-Sue laughed for ages. They are PROPER JOKES.

Mum asked who told me to write to Tilak's, so I said Mr Brightwell, my careers advisor. Mum just tutted and said, 'Huh, your careers advisor!' Then she said that's where she went wrong in the Eighties, listening to do-gooders like that and if she had her days to live over again she'd have just married someone with cash. Dad's face brightened when she said that, like he was imagining it. Mum says that Collette Brown from Cheeky's has got the right idea. She'll get herself set up with some bloke with a bit of dough like one of them WAGs. She won't be working in that tanning place long.

Cava-Sue tutted when she said that. Probably 'cos her Lewis goes round looking like a homeless. Mum says if I had any sense I'd get myself a builder or someone who is a bit handy 'cos she's always wanted the kitchen knocked through into the utility room and one of them breakfast bars like Carrie's mum has got – except tasteful.

I said I would try.

FRIDAY 14TH MARCH

CARRIE STILL BEING BLANKED BY BEZZIE – There

are only so many fake faces of disappointment that I can pull whenever Carrie mentions it.

Ms Bracket asked if anyone wanted any help with our work placement letters today as she was happy to assist. I showed her my letter to Tilak's and she looked at it and smiled a bit then got out her red pen. There is never any time at Mayflower when a red pen means anything good.

Ms Bracket says that she is very impressed by my vocabulary but sometimes 'less is more' when it comes to writing a job application letter. She reckons that I don't need to tell Mr Tilak all about how unique or mental I am or how I would cause lots of friction at the factory, as it's not like applying for *Big Brother* – they like people to be quiet.

Ms Bracket says I might be a bit bored putting pakoras into boxes – why don't I look for a placement that stretches me a bit, like at Essex FM radio or the *Ilford Bugle* newspaper, something where having a lively personality and a bright wit would be a good thing? That sounded much more exciting but I couldn't be arsed to start the letter again from the beginning so I'm not going to bother.

'What you need to remember, Shiraz Bailey Wood,' she said and looked straight into my eyes, 'is that you are the master of your own destiny.'

I don't know what that meant. I reckon it's something off *Star Wars*.

## SUNDAY 16TH MARCH

Today was proper weird. I don't think I can write about about it now.

## WEDNESDAY 19TH MARCH

Right, so here goes. So on Sunday, me and Carrie are sitting in her bedroom on her massive bed eating a big bag of Cheesy Starships and watching *Soccer Idol* on Sky One, which we totally only watch for the bits where the boys go in the post-match showers and you nearly see their willies, then Carrie's phone beeps and it's a text from a number we don't recognize. The message is: WOT U UP2? JUST PICKED UP YOUR BEBO MESSAGE. WANNA CM OVA? – BEZZIE

So Carrie looks at me and at first she can't speak and then she runs up to the mirror and starts shovelling on lipgloss and glitter eye-makeup and trying to find her best scrunchy and her thick gold charm bracelet while making a noise a bit like a fire alarm, and at first I don't know what's going on but then I finally get the gist of things and even though I've been dreading this happening I can't help but feel excited as Carrie says we are going to Bezzie's house!!! Deep down I have been dying to see what is behind the front door on Dawson Drive, considering I've heard about it so many times in Bezzie's track 'Who Got Da Beef?'. There's a bit where Bezzie raps:

'Roll up at my yard you'll check nuffin' finer.

I'll bring ya' cup of tea in my finest chin-a.

I'll bring ya ice bay-be. I'll wine ya. I'll dine ya.

I'll spit you some bare rhymes on my IKEA recliner.'

Personally, I think this is the crappest rap in the world ever. Who drinks tea in finest china? How old is he, thirty?

Carrie, however, thinks Bezzie's lyrics are proper sick and even suggested to Ms Bracket that we study 'Who Got Da Beef?' as poetry for English as a GCSE set text instead of that Siegfreid Sassoon geezer who waffles on about getting shot at in the Second World War, which Carrie says is too upsetting.

So we roll up at Bezzie's yard and knock on the door and I swear I can almost hear Carrie's heart thumping through her T-shirt, and Bezzie opens the door and he's got on white Nike tracksuit bottoms and a blue Adidas T-shirt and a little gold hoop earring, and the first thing I thought was how bloody enormous he was as he must be six foot three. I also thought how thin he was and what a huge nose he had, but later on Carrie said that she will always remember how gorgeous he was and how pale blue his eyes were and how he said, 'Come in ladies, lovely to meet you,' when he didn't say that at all, he said, 'Gnnngnnnn'right? Come in, mind the mutt.' Then a King Charles Spaniel called Shane which was about a hundred years old limped out of the living-room and licked us both and gave us a paw and Bezzie's mum shouted shut the door 'cos we were causing a draught.

Bezzie's bedroom wasn't a whole lot different to our Murphy's. It was sort of messy and there was a funny smell of feet and Lynx Wildebeest bodyspray and posters on the wall out of *Nuts* magazine of naked women covering their boobs and their mufties with their hands. Bezzie's mum must have a 'no mufty and nipple on the wall' rule too like my mum. There was quite a lot of posters of cars and stuff ripped out of car magazines too and all over the floor there was wires and recording equipment and a microphone set up as if it was a studio as well as a bedroom. Oh and lots of socks and cups and crisp packets. Anyway, I'm forgetting the main thing. Sitting on the bed watching *Time Team* on Bezzie's portable telly was a lad with brown hair and blue eyes in a hoodie and jeans.

It was Wesley Barrington Bains II!

'Y'all right?' I said to him, then I did my best face which said: look mate, I'm not bothered 'bout you, I'm just here with Carrie, right?'

I wanted him to know that I know that I'm not good-looking or anything and have no boobs and flat nipples and look a bit like a lemon so I didn't want him to think I had any silly ideas about him just 'cos his mate liked mine.

'Y'all right?' he said. Then he smiled at me and he had a nice smile. My stomach felt funny like I needed the loo or something. It was probably all those Cheesy Starships 'cos they ain't exactly complex carbohydrate. Wesley had lovely green eyes and wasn't at all fat up close. He's about seventeen and he looks like a proper bloke, he's got wide shoulders and a bit of hair coming out of his T-shirt top, not that I was looking that much. I sat down on the bed beside him and he smelled a bit of Adidas sports deodorant and we both watched that little bloke off *Time Team* with the specs dig up a plate which proved beyond doubt that people in the olden days had plates.

Anyway, the good thing was that Bezzie and Carrie seemed to hit it off dead well 'cos she started asking him all about EXACTLY how they record their tracks, so Bezzie started showing her the mic and the DAT recorder and how they host their MP3s online. Eventually Wesley said to me, 'You at Mayflower, innit?'

And I said, 'Yeah.'

And he said, 'Are you, like, one of them superchavs innit??'

And I tutted and said, 'No mate. You wanna check your mouth tho', being so prejudicial.'

And he laughed proper loud then and I rolled my eyes at him and folded my arms. Then he said, 'Do you live nearby?'

And I said, 'What you wanna know that for, bruv? Gonna stalk me?'

And he laughed well loud again and said 'No'.

That last bit was meant to sound like a joke, but when I think about it, I sounded like I reckoned I was a rudegirl. A bit like when I told Eric he had brain damage. Me and Carrie stayed for an hour and then we went home.

Bezzie never tried to kiss Carrie or nothing and he never even said he'd send her a text, but on our way home Carrie said that she felt like her life will never be the same again EVER. It is Wednesday night now and Bezzie hasn't texted or nothing but Carrie says she knows he will as it is DESTINY.

I went to bed on Sunday night and I couldn't sleep and when I did drop off I dreamed that Wesley Barrington Bains II was coming round and Cava-Sue was trying to put a tiara in my hair and it kept dropping out and smashing on Mum's new breakfast bar.

I am never eating Cheesy Starships again.

# APRIL

## WEDNESDAY 2ND APRIL

EASTER BREAK. IT'S SO BORING 'COS I AM TOTALLY SKINT. I asked Mum for hard cash, she got me a Twix egg instead.

I am also bored 'cos Carrie is TOTALLY IN LOVE with Bezzie Kelleher. Yeah, OK, she's been in love with him since January, but she says it's MUCH deeper now that she's actually spoken to him. Carrie's been over to Bezzie's house two times over the last fortnight to listen to some of his new tracks. Carrie doesn't really want to listen to Bezzie's tracks, she wants to snog him and stick her hands up his T-shirt and nibble his ears, but Bezzie ain't exactly all over her like an octopus in return.

It's all a bit weird. Bezzie keeps texting Carrie and saying come over, then when she gets there covered in lipgloss and glitter makeup with her hair all GHD'd and her best hoodie on, stinking of Still by J-Lo Eau de Parfum, then Bezzie just sticks on some MP3 of a track he laid down that day at his Sound Engineer NVQ course, then they sit on his IKEA futon and eat Breville toasted sandwiches. Bezzie likes cheese string and baked bean ones.

I asked Carrie if she has even properly snogged with

Bezzie yet and she said no, not really, although he did try to give her a Chinese burn the other night when they were messing about and there was a 'definite electric voltage' running between them. Carrie says she knows that Bezzie is a 'man with needs' and she knows he has a 'great passion bubbling away beneath his layers, aching to erupt'. I think she means under his shell-suit bottoms. Can't say I noticed it myself.

(I prefer to think that beneath Bezzie's shell-suit bottoms he has ANOTHER pair of shell-suit bottoms then welded-on underpants 'bubbling away', 'cos the thought of him naked puts me off my fishfingers.)

Carrie thinks Bezzie is 'sex on a stick'. Carrie has never been the same since she finished *The Princess Diaries* on Day One of her holidays to Dominican and ended up reading her mother's Jackie Collins novel which was full of proper filthy bits about people doing it non-stop. Carrie wants to get a grip of herself or Latoya will be calling her a hoochie slut too.

Carrie reckons the problem with Bezzie is he's a bit shy. I don't. I reckon he is a bit gay. On the *Nine O' Clock News* once I saw a film about a 'gay pride' march in central London and not all gays looked like Sean Burton in our class with the streaks who likes Kylie Minogue. Some of them looked like Bezzie too. Carrie didn't look very happy when I said this and sat with her bottom lip out all through English, looking a lot like a baby pigeon.

I can't help it if I tell the truth. This is what I was meaning in my careers talk. This is why I'd be dead good on *Big Brother*. I can't keep stuff in my head, it just blurts out of my mouth. I ain't changing for nobody. I am too real.

## THURSDAY 3RD APRIL

I've been thinking. Maybe I do need to stop blurting stuff out. I don't reckon Bezzie is gay really. He's probably just a bit scared 'cos Carrie keeps turning up at his house with big streaks of blusher down her face and glitter eyeshadow that makes her look like one of them New Zealand tribesmen who wait at the airport with spears to scare Prince Charles. I won't tell Carrie this. I'll keep it to myself.

I'll never make 2.2 million quid like Tabitha Tennant if I keep on being this thoughtful.

## SATURDAY 5TH APRIL - EASTER SATURDAY

This morning Carrie rang me and told me to tart myself up as we were meeting Bezzie and Wesley at 2.30pm. So I said, 'Carrie, I DON'T WANNA meet Wesley.'

And she said, 'Well it's not like a proper date or nuffin', more like hanging out together in a four.'

So I said, 'Well what do I get out of that?!'

And she said, 'Oh come on Shizza, be a mate.'

So it turns out that Carrie really wants to see Bezzie and vice versa, but Bezzie has promised Wesley that he'd hang out with him this Saturday 'cos Wesley had the day off at Argos where he works part time in the storeroom when he's not doing his NVQ2 in Plumbing. So anyway, Bezzie was meeting Wesley and they were going to cruise about in Bezzie's Vauxhall Nova and show off his new chrome exhaust and Carrie wanted to ride with them too.

So I said again, 'Yeah Carrie, but why do you need me there?' So Carrie said well 'cos I'm her BEST FRIEND IN THE WHOLE WORLD of course, but also 'cos her dad, Barney, was giving her 'nuff grief about seeing Bezzie and he doesn't want Carrie going around in Bezzie's car, so Carrie wanted me to come over to Draperville and pretend we're both going to Vue Multiplex to see *Hopeless In Love* starring Lindsay Lohan, but we weren't really, we were meeting Bezzie and Wesley in Fatty Arbuckle's car park and going for a ride.

So I said to Carrie, 'So you want me to lie to your father?'

And Carrie said, 'Oh get you, goody-two-shoes, what about last week when I had to back up your story to your mother about those Niko trainers getting stolen in PE when you really sold them to the Bean twins' big sister for a tenner?'

I shut up then and stuck some lipgloss on and my big parka with the fluffy hood and my big hoop earrings and decided to go and meet her.

Barney wasn't in when I got to Draperville, but Maria, Carrie's mum, was. Maria was in the lounge area by their big dinner table arranging loads of orchids that she'd bought from Asda into a big glass vase. Carrie's mum was asking me all about the movie we were going to see and I felt proper terrible about lying to her as Maria is a nice woman. I felt even worse when she gave us a tenner Easter money to spend on popcorn and hot-dogs. Carrie nearly pulled my arm off dragging me to Fatty Arbuckle's as quick as she could.

When we got there, Bezzie and Wesley were parked up in the disabled space and they beeped their horn and we got in. Wesley turned round in the front seat and smiled at me and said, 'All right Shiraz?'

So I said 'Yeah' and looked out of the window and blew a big Bazooka gum bubble while Carrie stuck her head through the seats and gave Bezzie a kiss, which he looked a bit shocked at.

We set off into Ilford and I stuck my seatbelt on and made Carrie fasten her one too, even though there wasn't much danger as we never went much over twenty-one miles an hour and there were old people my nan's age passing us on shopmobility scooters.

When we got into Ilford town centre Bezzie rolled down the windows and flipped on the CD player and stuck on one of the G-Mayes Detonators' new tracks called 'Gun Bumpin' which Bezzie told me and Carrie was all about how guns are dead bad and are totally destroying society. The chorus went like this:

'Brap-brap-brap boi

Am gun bumpin.

Brap brap brap –

a got da crowd jumpin –

Brap brap brap – got gun fingers frontin'

Got ma gun in your mouth – now ya no dis boi is sumfin'.'

Bezzie turned up the volume dead loud so it was blasting out of the boot and the entire car was shaking and my ears were crackling. People in the street were giving us funny looks as we drove along and some people were smirking. They obviously couldn't work out that the Detonators' track was AGAINST guns not FOR them. That's the thing about grown-ups, they just judge you and act prejudicial without even checking the facts out proper. I hope I'm never like that when I grow up. I hope I never just look at some young people and go, 'Ugh, chavs!' just 'cos they're wearing a hoodie or a Burberry scarf or listening to loud music. I'm not going to turn into a boring old fart who stereotypes everyone like grown-ups do. I'm the master of my own destiny after all, as Ms Bracket said.

For the next hour we drove around the one-way system in Ilford very slowly, beeping horns at other people that Bezzie and Wesley knew who were driving Citroën Saxos and Ford Orions. We couldn't talk to each other 'cos the music was so loud, but it was well exciting.

Eventually Bezzie said he was hungry and Carrie said she was too and they both said they wanted a Burger King and I said, 'Well I'm not hungry,' and so did Wesley 'cos he'd just eaten two Pepperamis and a big packet of Cadbury's mini-eggs. Then – before I knew what was happening – I'd been dropped off at the far side of Goodmayes with Wesley Barrington Bains II standing beside me on the kerb and Carrie shouting that she would text us and pick us up in half an hour as her and Bezzie wanted some 'quality time' alone. THEN THEY DROVE OFF!

I looked at Wesley and he looked at me then he burst out laughing. 'Your mate is a mentalist,' he said, shaking his head. I didn't know what to say 'cos I was really angry and dreaming up some sort of bad revenge against Carrie for dropping me, like telling Wesley to tell Bezzie that Carrie got her period last year at Laserquest when she was wearing white jeans and had to walk back with her hoodie wrapped round her mufty area 'cos she looked like something off *Texas Chainsaw Massacre*. Then I decided to just go home and blank Carrie's calls.

'Chill out, Shiraz. They'll be back soon anyway, innit?' said Wesley. I just tutted and folded my arms. I didn't say a word for about a minute 'cos I was raging. ''Ere, do you wanna watch Channel U at mine for a bit?' he said. 'I only live on the next cul-de-sac.'

I looked at him and rolled my eyes. 'Yeah, 'spose,' I said.

We walked along the road together at first saying nothing, then Wesley said, 'Oi, y'know, I been thinking about that superchav stuff I said about Mayflower when I first met you. Sorry Shiz, I was out of order.'

So I shrugged and I said, 'No worries mate.'

And he said, 'I was only saying it 'cos that's what the boys on my plumbing NVQ call Mayflower, y'know, "Superchav Academy"?'

I couldn't help smiling then and I said, 'Oh bring it on bruv, I've heard it all.' And then I said, 'It's sweet being a superchav really.' Then we both laughed for ages and chatted about the Brunton-Fletchers down my road 'cos they ARE superchavs.

So we went to Wesley's house and his car was sitting outside in the drive – it's a Golf and it's banana-yellow with a big spoiler on the back. We went into his house through the back door into the kitchen. It was proper clean and modern and tidy with no clutter. 'Minimalist' as my mum would say. 'I want our gaff to be minimalist!' she always says when she sees it on *Sixty Minute Makeover*. My mum could never be minimalist, she'd have to get rid of all that horse brass that Nan gave her and her porcelain Victorian figurine collection that she built up month by month out of the *News of The World* magazine and the millions of copies of *Chat*, *Pick Me Up* and *Sky TV* magazine that she always eats her tea off, and worst of all Murphy, who is not minimalist at all, because he is a giant who smells of farts.

Anyway, Wesley's house hasn't got any of this clutter. It's all cream carpet and white formica and no fuss. I asked him if his mum and dad were home and he said his mum was at work 'cos she works in admin at Romford ice rink, and then he didn't mention his dad so I reckon he ain't got one. Then we found a note on the side from his mother saying: *Wes – if you're home about 5pm can you stick the oven on 200 and shove a spud in for me?* and Wesley rolled his eyes and laughed and said, ''Ere Shiraz, make sure you remind me,' and I said I would.

We sat in the lounge, him on the chair and me on the couch and watched *Bliss* and Channel U and I tried to just watch the new Killa Kela video and not look at Wesley much as I kept thinking he had well nice green eyes and there was something sort of kind about him that I'd never noticed before. We were reading out the text messages on the screen and laughing and talking about how being locked up in jail always looks like a good laugh on Channel U 'cos you spend all your time weightlifting and doing dance routines, which we both know isn't true, 'cos you spend your time wanting to get out.

I was having a really good time then, 'cos Wesley is well easy to talk to for a boy. Then Carrie and Bezzie turned up, and Carrie said that me and her should go back to Draperville 'cos her dad would be looking for her. As we left I said, ''Ere Wesley, remember that spud.'

And he winked and tapped his nose and said, 'It's all in order, Shizza.'

Then I said 'See ya' and I left the house and my heart was thumping like mad and I felt a bit sick again.

On the way up the road Carrie was twittering on and on and on about Bezzie Kelleher and how totally wonderful and amazing he is, and how she wants to go to a car cruise in Southend with him, and then she said, ''Ere Shiz, do you fancy Wesley Barrington Bains II at all yet?'

And I just laughed at her and said 'No way' 'cos I don't.

## WEDNESDAY 9TH APRIL

Tilak Foods
Unit 57
Bishop Fledding Industrial Estate
Goodmayes
Essex
IG5 9PH

Dear Miss Wood
We are pleased to inform you that we can offer you a work placement at Tilak Foods this summer, monitoring and spectating on the daily work at our factory.

The dates we can offer are 2nd to 13th June.

The working hours will be from 8am until 4.30pm.

A minibus service is available from the town centre to transport you to the factory. Please see attached page for times and collection points.

Please can you confirm, as soon as possible, that these dates are suitable.

Yours sincerely

Kashaf Reman – PA to Mr Tilak

SUNDAY 14TH APRIL

Got up at 11am today and Mum had gone with Dad to Allied Carpets to get some new lino for the kitchen and Cava-Sue was still out at her mate Luella's and Carrie was at her nan's and Murphy was at Tariq's and I had no one to talk to aside from the dog and I was totally bored and for some reason kept thinking about Wesley Barrington Bains II. I dunno why. I just kept thinking it would be good to see him and watch Channel U with him again – just as a mate, nothing else – which is stupid 'cos I don't even know him. In the end I thought I might as well have a go at my English coursework 'cos Ms Bracket has been right on my case recently and I can't be dealing with her 'cos I think she must have OCD or high-functioning Aspergers or something 'cos she is OBSESSED with GCSEs. The coursework was a topic Ms Bracket keeps going on about all the time which is 'writing to argue, pursuade and advise'.

'This is a vital part of the curriculum!' she keeps saying.

Basically we had to think of an imaginary situation like a nightmare holiday, then write an argument to the manager arguing our point. 'This should be right up your street, Shiraz Wood!' Ms Bracket said and winked at me. I gave her one of my best 'Uma' looks.

So anyway, I went into Murphy's room and used the computer to type. It turns out our computer ISN'T AS BROKEN as Murphy makes out and the printer still works and the dial-up connection is bloody fine. MURPHY IS A TOTAL LIAR. I looked at Wesley's Bebo for a while. He looks dead sexy in some of his pics.

Anyway, it took me ages to do this coursework 'cos it is all totally imaginary, but I think it's not bad.

Dear Mr Manager
Re: Club Coco Loco, Tenerife
I am writing to complain and advise about a holiday that I have just spent in your Club Coco Loco, Tenerife, with my mate, Carrie, in July this year.

I have just spent two weeks of <u>sheer unmitigated hell</u> in a half-finished hotel, what was advertised as 'the most stunning jewel in the crown of this fabulous island'. Well if this is your most stunning jewel mate, you ain't got much bling bruv, 'cos this place was a right state and you are a proper liberty sending anyone there.

Lots of things jacked me off but the main one is that there were no facilities whatsoeva. Those gyms and golf course you were giving it the big one about are still covered in cement mixers. And there are workmen everywhere with their hairy bum clefts hanging out of their trousers. Minging.

And the so-called shopping mall was just a few old Spanish duffers selling a right load of old tat out of barrows. I've seen better stuff in the bins after Walthamstow market.

We was warned by the woman in the travel shop that the weather could be 'changeable'. That's one way of putting it. It pissed it down for a fortnight. And a further reason I am narked right off is that we flew from Manchester up north 'cos the flights were meant to be cheaper than Gatwick, then it was delayed so we missed nearly a day of our holiday sitting in Manchester Airport's departure lounge which was full of northerners all talking in weird voices about *Coronation Street* and eating egg sandwiches what they had brought from home.

This brings me to my next area of complaint. The hotel food. There was nothing I liked apart from the cheese croquettes and the curry sauce. Your brochure stated food was 'plentiful and traditional' and that it was available day and night. Well they stopped the croquettes at 8pm so that weren't true either, WAS IT?

But the thing we are most livid about is the 'nightlife'. It said in the brochure there was 'nightlife to suit all tastes'. Well yeah, if your taste is getting off with some forty-year-old munter and dancing to ten-year-old UK garage then you will be well sorted, mate. Me and my mate Carrie ended up playing Travel Connect Four every night and even Carrie couldn't find no one to get off with and believe me she ain't fussy.

Therefore, after having endured two weeks of this ordeal, I feel that I and my friend are deserving of at least a sizeable compo claim or we will be forced to take this matter further and may release our photographs to that Nicky Campbell bloke off *Watchdog* who will expose you for the right bunch of cowboys that you are.

Yours sincerely

Shiraz Bailey Wood

## MONDAY 15TH APRIL

BACK TO SCHOOL – I gave Ms Bracket the 'writing to argue, pursuade and advise' coursework today at the beginning of class, then we all sat down and read some war poetry by ourselves while Ms Bracket did some marking. It was quiet for a while then suddenly Ms Bracket started to laugh. Everyone looked up 'cos Ms Bracket don't laugh that much. She is usually well serious. It was really nice to see her face all lit up like a lightbulb, she looked all young again, and she isn't, she's about thirty-three. She tried to stop herself laughing by putting her hands in her face, then she started again even louder and her head went back and her mouth opened and I could see her silver fillings. Then eventually she said, 'Excuse me please, class 10W,' and she walked into the corridor and we could all hear her howling like a mad woman outside. Eventually she came back in with a serious face again and sat down and got her red pen out.

At the end of the class as I was leaving Ms Bracket called me over and gave me back my 'writing to argue' homework. She says if I take out the swearing and slang words and 'double negatives' and sort out some of the spelling she'll give me an A–.

I am not telling anyone like Carrie or Kezia or Luther about it 'cos it'll get around the class and I'll get called a swot and a suck-ass but I am WELL HAPPY.

## THURSDAY 18TH APRIL

Carrie came round tonight and we sat in the kitchen and watched *EastEnders* on Mum's kitchen telly and ate ice-pops and talked about Kezia Marshall's new hair 'cos she tried to dye it 'raunchy auburn' last night when it's ginger and it's gone a bit green at the sides and some of the lads are calling her swampbeast.

Carrie says that Bezzie and Wesley are DEFINITELY going to a car cruise in Southend next Friday night and am I gonna come, 'cos she could tell her dad she's coming here and I could tell my mum I'm at Draperville and then as long as no mums ring each other we'll be sweet. I said no. I said I don't wanna go to a car cruise 'cos I don't like riding about in cars 'cos I get carsick.

This wasn't true. I do like riding about in cars but I am still fizzing with Carrie for leaving me on the kerb near Wesley's house that Saturday. I think that was totally disrespectful to me as a mate and I certainly don't wanna get dumped in Southend if she does it again. Carrie would NEVER EVER do anything like that usually. She is a top girl and my best friend ever since Year Seven. This is all since she met Bezzie Kelleher. Sometimes I feel like she likes Bezzie almost as much as she likes me and it freaks me out.

'Oh come on Shiz, it'll be such a laugh! Three hundred cars are coming from all over Essex!' she said. 'They do burn-outs and donuts and stuff!'

'I can get donuts at Asda,' I said.

'Not them sort of donuts,' she said.

We sat and said nothing for a while.

'God, Shiraz, you've really got bad vibes about Wesley Barrington Bains II, ain't you?' Carrie said.

'I ain't got NO vibes about Wesley Barrington Bains II!' I said, then my mum came in, probably to change the batteries on her sonic ear trumpet that she uses to find out everything that happens in Goodmayes ever.

'Wesley Barrington Bains II?' said my mum.

'Gnnnnno,' I grunted, then I stared at the telly.

'You know him, do you?' she said.

'Yeah a bit,' said Carrie. I scowled at Carrie to shut up.

'I knew Wesley Barrington Bains the First,' said Mum. 'He used to come in the social club all the time, terrible nice fella he was. Mad keen on cars.'

I tried to pretend I wasn't listening but I totally was.

'What happened to him?' said Carrie.

'Oh . . . it was a terrible business,' said Mum. 'He was indoors one day looking after his little lad, right as rain, then when his missus came home from work . . . he was laid out flat on the living-room floor, stone-cold dead! The little lad playing with his toys beside him. Heart attack! Only thirty-two he was. The little boy just thought he was sleeping. There was bloody hundreds down at that crematorium. Horses in plumes. The lot. They still live in that house y'know. Over near Dawson Drive.'

Mum grabbed a choc-ice out the freezer and disappeared back into the lounge.

Me and Carrie sat for a while and said nothing. I felt a bit raw in the back of my throat.

'Me and Bez reckon he likes you,' Carrie said.

'Oh shut up,' I said.

WEDNESDAY 23RD APRIL

I was really bored today at school 'cos I've totally lost track of what Mr Gilligan is going on about in Geography, then in Maths we were doing statistics and they are bleeding tedious. Then at break Carrie was going on about Bezzie and Southend again, then after lunch it was double Hockey and I thought, balls to this, I'm off home. So I walked, with Carrie and Kezia, in the general direction of PE, then as I got to the PE block I just kept walking past the changing-room door and out of the block and out of the back gates and down the road and on to the 239 bus towards home. The trick is all in your expression. Never EVER look like you shouldn't be going somewhere and usually you don't get stopped.

So I get home and I get into bed and reckon I'll have two hours' kip before Mum's due in from work, then I'll get up and walk round the block and come home at the same time as ever. EASY. So I'm just drifting into a nice dream (about Wesley, if you must know) when the front door opens downstairs! MY HEART NEARLY STOPPED. So I pull the whole duvet over my head and a few pillows too and try to stop breathing 'cos if it's Mum she will kill me with her bare hands 'cos I have promised on Nan's life to her I won't skive any more since the Year Nine exclusion.

Then I hear Cava-Sue go, 'Nah, there's never anyone here during the day,' and Lewis go, 'Are you sure? 'Cos your mum will go mad if you're skiving as well as scrounging off the state.' Then they both laugh. Now the thing is, even though Cava-Sue is skiving, if she finds out I'm skiving I KNOW she'll grass me up at some other time and I'll still get killed, so I crouch in a ball and play dead.

They both came upstairs and they're laughing and

talking about college and going down Blackhorse Road to their mate's flat then going to a pub in Camden, then they fall through the bedroom door and I should have shouted then, 'LOOK!! CAVA-SUE, I'M HERE, ALL RIGHT!!' but I didn't 'cos I wanted to earwig on them a bit more, but then – AND THIS IS THE REALLY REALLY BAD BIT – I hear them both climbing up the bunk-bed ladder and getting into bed and all I could hear then was them snogging and making squelchy sounds and through the crack in the duvet I saw Cava-Sue's leopard-skin bra go flying past on to the floor, then the bunk bed BEGAN TO SHAKE and Lewis was making a sort of asthmatic sound and Cava-Sue was going, 'Yeah! Ooh! Yeah! Oooooooh Lewy!' and I buried my head under all the covers and felt really really vomitous and I wish I could wash my brain in Domestos 'cos the sound of them doing whatever they were doing will be with me until the DAY THAT I DIE.

CAVA-SUE – I WISH YOU WOULD MOVE OUT.

## FRIDAY 25TH APRIL

I still cannot look at Cava-Sue without feeling ill.

Carrie is going to Southend tonight. I've told her that she better not say she's at mine 'cos if Barney rings I'm not saying she's popped to the chippy and has her mobile off again as he knows full well I'm faking. Carrie says she won't. I'm glad I'm not going. It sounds rubbish anyhow.

Just loads of sitting about. Carrie says Wesley will be sad I'm not coming 'cos he asked Bezzie to ask Carrie if I was going to come tonight. I know this isn't true. This is just Carrie making stuff up to make me feel like less of a cling-on with her and Bezzie. I know Wesley would never be bothered about what someone like me was doing. I know he probably doesn't even remember that day with Channel U and the baked potato and the superchav conversation. Not like I do anyhow.

## SATURDAY 26TH APRIL

I didn't get out of bed much today.

## SUNDAY 27TH APRIL

Carrie rang me yesterday morning and said the car cruise in Southend was blinding. Carrie said there was loads of people there doing burn-outs and donuts and the police turned up and everything. Carrie said Wesley Barrington Bains II turned up by himself. Carrie said he hung about by himself for most of the night 'cos Carrie was with Bezzie.

Carrie said in the end Wesley met a girl called Dee-Dee from Romford who has blonde hair and big boobs and a neon-blue Golf with glowing wheel arches. Carrie said he snogged her.

When Carrie told me this I put the phone down

and then I put my *Hip Hop Divas* album on and then
I got into bed and curled my arms round my knees and
then I cried.

# MAY

## THURSDAY 1ST MAY

I haven't seen Carrie much this week, except for at school and even then it's like she's in another world. It's all Bezzie and me did this and Bezzie and me did that and then me and Bezzie went to Burger King and then me and Bezzie went to Halfords and then me and Bezzie went to South Mimms Services and it was well jokes 'cos Bezzie bought us both Kinder Surprise eggs and then Bezzie made the toy and it was a frog in a rowing boat and we called it Cyril and then we drove home and the police gave us a dirty look at the traffic lights 'cos of Bezzie's exhaust pipe and that was proper hilarious and then Bezzie and then Bezzie . . . AND BELIEVE ME SHE CAN GO ON LIKE THIS ABOUT BEZZIE ALL BLOODY DAY LONG.

I miss the old Carrie Draper. Life is so crap right now.

## SATURDAY 3RD MAY

Carrie was with Bezzie today. I went on Bebo and updated my profile with some stuff about me 'Lovin Lif 2 the Max Rite Now + 4eva!!!' I am such a fake.

## THURSDAY 8TH MAY

Today Carrie asked me what was up at school 'cos she reckons I'm being a bit off with her and giving her evils so I said, 'Nah mate, I am so totally not giving you evils right?'

And Carrie said, 'Well have you got an issue or something 'cos then we need to communicate about it?'

And I said, 'Nah. And if I had something to say to you I'd say it to your face and not behind your back 'cos you're my friend.'

So Carrie said, 'OK Shiz, fair play. Maybe I'm just a bit paranoid 'cos I'm nearly on my period.'

Then we linked arms and went to lunch together and we had chips and curry sauce with loads of ketchup and iced buns 'cos it was Friday so they don't sell all that healthy option crap. We sat in the lunch hall and I tried to talk to Carrie about stuff other than Bezzie. It was hard.

At the end of school we both walked home sharing her iPod and having a laugh, but when I got back home I realized she'd not even asked me what I was doing this weekend at all.

## SATURDAY 10TH MAY

NO phonecall off Carrie! Went on to my Bebo and clicked on to Carrie's page to check out any new pics she has up. That's when I noticed something that REALLY DID MY HEAD IN. Until recently, Carrie's main picture was of me and her at Draperville messing about with strawberry sauce all over our faces with the message:

Heya every1!!!! Urm i dno wt 2 say in these things!! Im Carrie. Im 15! quite random! Choclite brown hair! U cn c frm my pics wt i look like!! I lurve you Shiraz Shiz Shoz Shizza! Complete legend. Lurve all the crap we do 2getha. WE RULE MAYFLOWER. SUPERCHAV ACADEMY 4EVA – he he he he NOT Rilly!!!! :D:D:D:D■D- nowt else 2 say! leave me a msg nd ill chat 2 ya l8rz CARRIExXxxXx

But now it says:

hey every1!!! So u no this is me Carrie! He he he!!!!. Bezzie Kelleher – OMG – you are my hunnybun . . . cldnt live wifout you in mi lf, we're eachothas sanity. I'm so glad I fnd u. Wen we go out we ave the bestest times . . . Southend Cruise omg hehehe!! love u more dan nefink!!! Cyril the Frog I luv him too!!! G-MAYES DETONATORS know yourselfs!!! I lurve you Shiraz Shiz Shoz too Complete legend. Lurve you 4eva xxxxxxxxxxxxxxxxxxxxxxxx

I looked at that for ages and felt totally gutted. Bezzie is FIRST and I am SECOND. Then I looked at Carrie's new pics. There were ones of her and Bezzie sitting on his bed. And one of them at South Mimms Services eating Kinder eggs. There were some of Wesley Barrington Bains II. He was sitting on the bonnet of a neon-blue car with his arm around a moody-looking girl who had longish straight white-blonde hair and huge knockers and a low-cut top on and loads of lipgloss. She was pretty, I suppose, in a well obvious Barbie way. It had to be Dee-Dee. Carrie has been hanging out with Wesley and Dee-Dee!

I switched the PC off and stormed downstairs and watched Channel U on my own. I must have looked sad 'cos when Murphy got home he made us both a banana Nesquick and let me win at Zombie Armageddon: Bloodbath II. I think I am depressed.

## SUNDAY 11TH MAY

I was meant to do my English coursework today, 'cos I totally promised Ms Bracket that I would, but I got up and thought WHAT IS THE POINT??

I'm not a suck-ass. I'm not going to pass English GCSE. That A– she gave me for 'writing to argue' was just a fluke. I don't need GCSEs anyway 'cos I'll work at Tilak's or somewhere for a bit until I go on *Big Brother* or whatever. I'm sick of thinking about all this crap. At about 2pm I went out to the shop to buy my mum some Pringles and a scratchcard and I bumped into Uma Brunton-Fletcher coming out of Kebabish and she said, 'Ya wanna come and cotch at mine?' and I said yeah.

Uma's house is scary. They've got no garden gate and a smashed-up front wall and a busted fridge by the front porch and the front door is boarded up 'cos the police kicked it in at New Year so you need to go around the back. Their kitchen is always full of randoms 'cos Uma's stepdad knocks out bags of skunk, so he's always sitting behind some electronic scales at the breakfast bar with a fag in his gob and a roll of clingfilm in his hand and there are always at least three brindle Staffies roaming about and kids and toddlers of different sizes everywhere and no carpet on the lounge floor.

So me and Uma went in the living-room and Uma got us both a Smirnoff Ice each, which I didn't really want but I didn't want to look soft. We sat on the couch and watched the DVD extras on *Homicidal Psychopath in Manhattan* where a woman was getting raped by a gang of axe-wielding thugs, and Uma said do I want a smoke, so I said yeah, even though I don't smoke. I had a few drags and a sip of my Smirnoff Ice and I started to feel proper sick.

Then Clinton arrived home from wherever he'd been, looking dead pale, and he plonked himself down beside me on the couch and he said, 'All right Shiz, not seen your mush for a while.'

And I said, 'Yeah, been busy.' 'Cos I couldn't tell him the truth that my mum says I'm not allowed in here 'cos they're all rough as hell.

Then Clinton said, ''Ere, do you know anyone that wants to buy an American Pit Bull puppy? I got its Kennel Club papers,' and I said no. Then he said, 'Do you know anyone who wants to buy a Taser?' and I said no and he said, 'Do you know anyone with size nine feet who likes

Ellesse trainers?' so I said no and then he left me alone.

After about three hours I went home and my mother said, 'Where have you been?' and I just grunted like it was none of her business and said 'Carrie's.' Check me out, I'm a superchav.

## WEDNESDAY 14TH MAY

Ms Bracket is livid about the English coursework. She started moaning on that I was 'just beginning to shine' and I'm 'wasting my potential'. She is mixing me up with someone who gives a crap.

Bezzie has bought Carrie a gold necklace with her name on it. Carrie wears it over the top of her school jumper and keeps playing with it all the time and looking mushy. Carrie reckons it means Bezzie is falling in love with her. If he was that in love he'd have got it from somewhere posh like H Samuels, not Argos where Wesley can get ten per cent staff discount.

## FRIDAY 16TH MAY

Carrie was going to the cinema tonight with Bezzie. They never invited me. I went round to Uma's and we walked over to the bandstand at Goodmayes Park where Kirky and Dazzle and Minno from Lowbridge Academy were. Dazzle had one of those mini-motorbikes that he'd borrowed off a kid on his estate and Uma brought some bottles of Blackcurrant Lambrella and we sat on the steps of the bandstand and ate chicken chow mein with our fingers and Uma texted everyone she knew to come over and meet us. Eventually Cassia and Ashleen came over who got excluded in Year Nine and ended up in Pupil Referral Unit and they brought Knighty from the unit, who's not allowed to come in the park at all now 'cos he's got an ASBO, but he still does 'cos he just keeps his hood up and tries to keep it on the low.

We hung around in the park for ages and Cassia and Ashleen were shouting stuff at anyone who went by and trying to get grown-ups to go into Londis and get them ten fags and more booze but no one would. Then some emo-gothy-type kids walked past who looked a bit like my Cava-Sue and her Lewis, and Cassia and Knighty were shouting all this nasty crap at them and I felt dead bad then 'cos I should have said something to stick up for them but I didn't 'cos I'm scared of Cassia 'cos she is a total rudegirl.

Then the park-keeper with the squashed strawberry nose and two policemen arrived together and one policeman told us to split into groups of no more than two and go home. Knighty made a swift exit 'cos of his behaviour order and so did Dazzle on the mini-bike, but Kirky and Cassia and Ashleen started getting all gobby and saying they had civil liberties and it started to get a bit lairy then 'cos Cassia was pretty hammered and saying all sorts of nasty stuff. Then the other policeman said he knew it was us who graffitied on the bandstand – which it TOTALLY WASN'T 'cos the graffiti was about a year old – and he said he could get Forensic down to prove it and put us in jail.

Then he swung round and said to me, 'And who are you? You're a new face.' And I nearly died of fright but I just did the same stare that Uma does and shrugged, so he said, 'What's your name?'

So I said, 'Veronica Fairish.'

And he said, 'Well Veronica, I want this to be the first and last time I ever meet you.'

Eventually Cassia and Uma agreed to disperse and as we walked home Uma was laughing and linking arms with me and saying, 'That was so wicked Shiz, you are a proper legend! Veronica Fairish! He he he!' And I walked along quietly and I felt crappy inside.

## SATURDAY 17TH MAY

I called Carrie this morning but she was going to Romford to look at some new wheel arches with Bezzie and Wesley. She asked me to go but she said Dee-Dee was going so I said no 'cos I'm not being a spare part. I lay in bed for ages and thought about her and Bezzie and how things have changed since he came along and I felt pretty sad. Then I thought about Wesley and his green eyes. Then I thought about that cow Dee-Dee and her huge boobs. Then I thought how different life might have been if I'd just gone to bloody Southend and maybe worn some glitter eyeshadow and inflated my tits with panty-pads. Then Uma texted me and said: WANNA GO2 THE MALL? and I thought: not really mate, 'cos you're a bit mental, but I couldn't think of a good way to put that in a text that wouldn't end up with a wheelie bin getting chucked through our window so I put on my McKenzie hoodie and my biggest hoops and went.

I met Uma outside KFC and she was with Cassia and Ashleen. Cassia was in a right strop 'cos she'd just tried to take some GHD straighteners back to Boots and they wouldn't give her even a credit note 'cos she didn't have a receipt or a box. The irons had all crispy burned hairspray on them like they'd been used loads of times.

Cassia was saying, 'So I said to her, you calling me a liar? Are you saying they weren't a gift?! You wanna know yourself disrespecting me like that!' Then Cassia said she was going to wait about until 6pm and give the silly bitch on the electrical counter a slap. I wasn't sure whether she was kidding or not, 'cos let's face it, Cassia ended up in Pupil Referral for headbutting Miss Coates.

We all walked off together into the mall and I wanted to go into Claire's Accessories to buy a scrunchy, but Uma said we couldn't 'cos she's on their central database of banned under-sixteens and it just causes loads of friction from the moment she goes in and that Triad security guard starts getting all up in her face. So we sat around on the wall by the plants for a while and I felt quite scared then 'cos Uma and Cassia kept getting into stupid arguments with passers-by who they accused of looking at them funny. Then Collette Brown from Cheeky's Vertical Tanning Salon walked by. She had a little cream leather jacket on over her white overall and perfect hair and high-heeled boots on. I waved and smiled at her but she just looked at me and looked embarrassed then walked off well quick. 'Who's that silly cow?' said Uma. 'She looks like a right slut.'

'Oh, no one,' I said. My cheeks were burning up.

Cassia stole two bright pink Rimmel Lycra Wear nail varnishes from Superdrug. She gave me them 'cos she's already got seven at home. She says stealing them is her new game. I went home as soon as I could. Cava-Sue was in the living-room ironing a dress for yet another night out in central London. Mum was in the kitchen slagging Cava-Sue off 'cos the dress was too short and had a rip in it and wasn't even new 'cos she'd got it second-hand off eBay.

'All right superchav? How's Uma?' Cava-Sue smirked as I walked past.

'OH SHUT UP, CAVA-SUE, YOU BLOODY SMELLY EMO-FREAK!' I shouted at her, then I stormed upstairs and slammed the door.

If Uma calls tomorrow I'm telling her I've been grounded until 2009.

Spent most of today in bed, with the dog under the duvet with me, reading *Heat* magazine and hoping Uma might forget I exist. Uma texted me THREE TIMES this afternoon seeing if I want to go to the Cash 4 Trash shop with her 'cos she'd 'found' a digital camera and she wanted to flog it and buy some booze and go to the park. I didn't want to go to Cash 4 Trash. It's full of heroin addicts pawning their tellies. I didn't want to go the park either 'cos that park-keeper with the strawberry nose looks proper depressed when he sees us. At about 6pm there was a knock at the front door and when I pushed my face to the window I NEARLY DIED WITH SHOCK. There was a police car outside my house!! My heart started jumping into my mouth and I ran around my bedroom trying to find those bloody stolen nail varnishes so I could hide them in the toilet cistern like they always do on *The Bill*.

My mother answered the door, then she shouted up the stairs, 'Shiiiiiiiiiraz! Come down here RIGHT NOW!' I walked downstairs shoving my hands into my pockets. I thought I might throw up.

'You ain't got Uma bloody Brunton-Fletcher up there with you, have you?' she said.

'No,' I said.

'See?' my mum said to the policeman. She looked at me. 'The police are looking for Uma again. That Clinton headcase has told them she'll be round here with you 'cos you're her mate. But you don't have nothing to do with Uma, do you?'

'No,' I said. I'm sure I looked like I was lying 'cos I was sweating like mad. I went back upstairs and got under the duvet and pulled it over my head.

I am officially retiring from being a superchav. I don't think there is much of a future in it.

But what now?

# JUNE

## MONDAY 2ND JUNE

Got up at 6am today to catch the minibus to Tilak Foods for my work experience. Tilak Foods is on an industrial estate in the middle of nowhere. I waited on the corner of Civic Close at 7am with a group of older women who were mostly Sikhs with long saris on under their anoraks. There were also some Eastern European women in stonewash denim jackets and ski pants and neon jumpers, plus some Somalian ladies too. There wasn't anyone my age on the bus at first, but after a few pick-ups a younger girl got on called Mercedes and we had to wait a minute while she finished her Lambert and Butler. I felt quite scared on the bus 'cos I didn't know anyone and no one talked to me. Without Carrie or Uma or Kezia I felt totally small and alone.

The Tilak factory is well big. As big as Mayflower Hockey Pitch used to be before it got sold. Tilak's is freezing cold inside. Especially near the fridges and freezers. There's a really pukey weird smell all the time, but it's not of bhajis or pakoras, it just smells like old chip fat. A bit like when Nan first got her deep-fat fryer and didn't change the lard in it for a year. Minging.

I went up to the office and a woman called Mrs Reman

met me and she said, 'You sixteen yet?' and I said, 'Nah, fifteen,' and she tutted and gave me a bag full of clothes and told me to get changed. I had to wear a big pair of white wellies, a hair-net over my hair, a dark red hat and a massive baggy dark red overall coat with white plastic buttons up the front. I looked in the toilet mirror and couldn't believe how much of a dog I looked. I put some lipgloss on to try and bootilicious myself up but when I got outside Mrs Reman said, 'Strictly no makeup,' and made me wipe it off with a rough hand-towel. Even bloody Mr Bamblebury the headmaster has given up on lipgloss.

The factory is proper noisy, you have to say everything twice. Today they were making lamb kofta balls. Basically, there's a big huge MASSIVE pan of mashed-up lamb gunk with a blade inside stirring it up and the mixture spits out a tube in the bottom into little balls. Then they go through an oven and then they plop out of the other end. My job today was observing the koftas being packed. You put six koftas in a box. Then six in another box. Then six in another box. Then when you've done six boxes they go into a much bigger box and you pull a lever and the box gets Sellotaped and sent off to get a label.

I watched this all day long. I must have seen nine hundred billion bloody koftas. The lady I was watching today was called Mrs Santosh Sandu. She was dead nice. Santosh says Tuesdays are much more exciting 'cos they make onion bhajis.

## TUESDAY 3RD JUNE

They make bhaji pretty much the same as you do kofta. Today was really boring. I counted to six all day. At 3pm Santosh let me pull the lever 'for a treat'.

## WEDNESDAY 4TH JUNE

Six in a box. One-two-three-four-five-six. Repeat six times. One-two-three-four-five-six. Pull the lever. One-two-three-four-five-six. I kept waking up in the night last night muttering and kicking and counting to six. Then I got out of bed sleepwalking to look for that bloody metal pole they use to stick up the chute and unblock the pakoras. Cava-Sue had to put me back into bed, then she sat on the side of my bunk for a while and held my hand just like she did when I was a little girl and I had bad dreams.

I think Tilak Foods is doing my head in.

## THURSDAY 5TH JUNE

HOW CAN IT BE ONLY THURSDAY? HOW!!!! I nearly chucked a sickie today but Cava-Sue stopped me. I spoke to Carrie on my lunchbreak. She is having a right old giggle at her work experience. Somehow she's working for her dad in the offices at Draper Hydration!! This is completely against the rules. Like I said, Mr Brightwell from the careers office is proper useless. For the first three days she just watched *Legally Blonde I* and *II* on her dad's new Mac Pro-book and tested out the whirlpool baths. I could do with a whirlpool bath. I smell like one big giant lamb kofta. Murphy says I stink like I should come with sauce and salad.

## FRIDAY 6TH JUNE

Santosh and all the other ladies were in a happier mood today 'cos they got paid. I found out that the pay at Tilak's is £5.50 an hour. That is almost £11,800 a year. I asked Santosh how much that was a week and she said £188.97 after income tax and national insurance. I asked her what that was and she laughed and said, 'If you don't know I envy you.'

£188.97? That sounds like quite a lot. I told my mother and she said, 'Yeah, but you'd be giving me at least £50 a week for your lodgings, I'm not having two of you BLOODSUCKERS bleeding me dry.' Then Cava-Sue gave Mum a filthy look and then they started swearing at each other about money and Cava-Sue getting 'above herself'. They were getting on so well this week too.

## SATURDAY 7TH JUNE

Me and Carrie went to Vue Cinema today to see *Oh My Gosh I Love Him!!* starring the Olsen Twins. It was Barney

Draper's treat to cheer Carrie up after a long week at work. A LONG WEEK AT WORK? HA HA HA! Excuse me while I die laughing. Carrie admitted that on Friday her and her mother went to Cheeky's Vertical Tanning and Collette Brown did them both a special Extra-Brown Ten-Minute Onyx Spray-Tan. Carrie is now almost as brown as Mrs Obdulu who makes the bhajis at Tilak Foods AND MRS OBDULU IS FROM THE PEOPLE'S REPUBLIC OF CONGO.

*Oh My Gosh I Love Him!!* was really crap. Carrie thought it was amazing. She said it 'totally, like, showed what it's like to open your heart to someone'. I thought I was going to vom up when she said that. And not just 'cos I'd eaten about £4.47 worth of sherbet starships.

## MONDAY 9TH JUNE

Week Two at Tilak's. OH MY GOD I PROPER HATE IT HERE. I hate the way you have to be here exactly on 8am and not one minute later or you're in trouble and you can't even go for a wee or look at a text message or change your tampon without getting permission off two people and ticking it off on a clipboard. I hate the way you can't wear lipgloss or earrings to make you look less like a munter. I hate that there is nothing to think about all day long except the bhajis and the pakoras and whether the chute is blocked, and I hate the way everyone is quite sad all the time and complaining about the money and bitching about Mr Tilak and Mrs Reman in the office who they blame for everything. And I hate how the Sikh women think the Polish women are snobby and want their jobs for their Polish friends, and the Somalian women are quite depressed and one of them called Farah Garaad bursts into tears a lot 'cos she misses her sons and wants them to come here to England from Mogadishu but they can't because they're in a war. I've sort of made friends with Mercedes, who is about twenty-six, but her sense of humour is well mucky and she keeps asking me if I am a virgin and accusing me of being a lezzer.

I stared at the clock from the moment I got there today and I swear it took SIX TIMES as long to go round to 4pm. I MISS MAYFLOWER ACADEMY.

## TUESDAY 10TH JUNE

At lunch today I sat at the vending machine with Mercedes. She asked me if I was coming back to Tilak's for a job next year and I said, 'Maybe. But just for a bit until I'm old enough to do *Big Brother.*' Mercedes laughed then and said that she wants to do *Big Brother* too. Mercedes says she always takes a sickie each year to go to the big audition in Victoria Dock in London, but there's always about five thousand folk there and you stand in the rain all day and she never gets past the first set of questions, which is totally unfair as she's got a lot to offer and would bring all sorts of 'controversialitiness' to the house. Even I know that's not a word.

Mercedes says she's been at Tilak Foods eight years. Mercedes says it is the most money that she can earn with no GCSEs or anything. She's always skint. Mercedes still lives with her mum. I must have looked a bit sad then 'cos she said, ''Ere Shiraz, don't stress too much about *Big Brother*. They're always looking for people for TV shows!' Mercedes says she's applied next for a show called '*Fast-Track Family Feud*' on ITV2 where you all sit on a stage in front of an audience and discuss your family problems. I asked her if her family was having a feud and she said, 'Well not right now but probably soon 'cos my sister is a right dirty trollop.'

## THURSDAY 12TH JUNE

Oh god. At Tilak's today I was feeling proper baffled by what I AM GOING TO DO WITH MY LIFE 'cos believe me THIS IS NOT IT when all of a sudden Mrs Obdulu started making a weird sound and so did Farah Garaad and when I looked around, Adrianna, one of the Polish women, had her hands over her mouth and her face was quite green. 'It's a rat! A rat!' Farah was shouting and everyone started screaming and jumping up on chairs.

Then Mrs Obdulu shouted, 'Not on the floor, you silly women – in the bhaji!!' and we all crowded up to the chute where the bhajis were plopping out and Mrs

Obdulu held up one and it had A LITTLE FOOT STICKING OUT and as we looked closer you could see all the little bhaji balls were full of blood and guts and bits of snout and hair.

'Oh not again!' said Mercedes, then she ran to the wheelie bin and threw up.

'Oh lord!' shouted Mrs Obdulu. 'Someone has left the trap open last night and another rat has fallen into the pan!' And all of a sudden I began to feel really really sick. My eyes felt misty and I turned around and started to stagger across the factory floor and as far away from the chute as I could go. Then I stumbled out of the factory door and into the road and then I just went a bit mad and began to run down through the industrial estate and on to the main road and then I just kept on going and I thought I AM NEVER EVER GOING BACK THERE EVER AGAIN and I didn't even know where the hell I was and I just kept running and people were tooting their horns and shouting stuff at me from vans 'cos I looked like such a nutter in my wellies and hat.

Then suddenly a car pulled up beside me and I ignored it and kept on going and then a bloke's voice shouted, 'Oi! Shiraz! Is that you, innit?' but I ignored him and then the voice said, 'Shiraz! It's me innit!' and when I turned around it was a banana-yellow Golf and in the driver's seat was Wesley Barrington Bains II!

I stopped and my mouth fell open.

'Shiraz! What's wrong?' he shouted.

I couldn't speak.

'Do you want a lift home?' he said.

I nodded.

'Come on, get in,' he said.

I got in the car and it felt warm and safe and it smelled of magic tree air fresheners and then I started to cry and Wesley held my hand.

I told Wesley about the mashed-up rat. He took me to Burger King drive-thru and bought me a hot coffee with sugar in it 'cos he said it was good for shock then he drove me home to Thundersley Road.

I know he's with Dee-Dee now but I am so happy that I have him as a friend.

10pm – Wesley must have rang Carrie on the way home 'cos she turned up with a box of Quality Street green triangles. We sat on my bed and listened to *Hip Hop Divas*. Carrie says the world of work is a right old pain up the ass and she's thinking of staying on in Mayflower Sixth Form. I know what she means.

## THURSDAY 19TH JUNE

This is TOP SECRET but I am really happy to be back at Mayflower with Carrie and Luther and Kezia and Sean Burton and everyone. I was even pleased to see Ms Bracket. 'So how was the factory?' she asked when I walked into English.

'Totally wack,' I said.

And she laughed and said, 'Well let's do our best to keep you out of there, eh, Miss Wood?'

And I shrugged and said, 'Whatever.'

I gave in my English coursework today. The task was to write about a sad situation through the eyes of someone else and demonstrate 'empathy'. I wrote about a day-in-the-life of a Somalian woman who lives in Ilford who misses her sons in Mogadishu and has to pull dead rats' feet out of the bhaji mix all day.

## MONDAY 23RD JUNE

Ms Bracket said my coursework was 'very gritty and moving' and 'showed a lot of empathy'. I didn't even try that hard either. Ms Bracket gave me an A–. But I'm keeping that on a strictly need-to-know basis.

Only this diary needs to know.

# JULY

## TUESDAY 1ST JULY

I was eating a bowl of Coco-Chocko Clusters and watching a GM TV exclusive about Peter Andre's new dog kennel when Mum made a funny 'Ooh' sound. She was reading a card the postman had just brought.

'What?' I said.

'Very exciting news,' she said, then she lit up a Kensitas Club and got out her bright pink lipstick and began drawing on her mouth like she always does before work. 'We have been cordially invited,' Mum said in her best la-di-dah voice, 'to the Draper Hydration Summer Barbecue on July the twentieth'.

'Who has?' said Cava-Sue, who was reading a play and eating toast made from that disgusting birdseed bread that she buys herself these days.

'Mr and Mrs Wood plus children,' said Mum.

'What Draper barbecue?' I said, crossly. Carrie ALWAYS forgets to tell me stuff these days, she is so annoying. I bet Bezzie Kelleher knows.

'Am I invited?' said Murphy, excavating his nose.

'All the Wood children are invited,' said my mum, then she started to laugh. ''Ere Shiraz, aren't Maria

141

Draper's bashes a bit snooty? All fancy cocktails and that Japanese raw fish stuff?'

'A bit,' I said.

''Ere, well I'll have to ring up Aunty Glo and see if she can cut your dad's hair before we go. I'm not having him turning up looking like a badger.' Mum looked at the invite again. ''Ere, do you reckon they'll have all the outdoor whirlpool jacuzzi things going, like on *Footballers' Wives*? Shall I bring my bikini?'

I put down the Coco-Chocko Clusters, 'cos suddenly they felt like stones in my mouth. NO WAY ARE MY PARENTS GOING IN THE JACUZZI. My mother's boobs are all saggy like an African tribeswoman's and my dad's toes have a calcium deposit problem which makes his toenails grow like werewolves'.

If Dad fronts up in those orange Speedos I SWEAR TO GOD, DIARY, I WILL KILL MYSELF.

## WEDNESDAY 2ND JULY

Clinton Brunton-Fletcher has a new girlfriend. It is Latoya Bell from our school with the diamond face-stud and the Acceptable Behaviour Contract. Latoya's been quiet lately ever since Kezia kicked her ass, but she wasn't tonight 'cos Clinton had bought an old Audi and they were driving around and around Goodmayes yelling out the window at people walking home from school. They called me 'Moose', and Carrie 'Big tits'. Bezzie was fuming when Carrie rang him. Bezzie said he was going to go round and give Clinton a slap. Then Bezzie worked out who Clinton was and said that violence wasn't the answer and he'd just diss him in the G-Mayes Detonators' new track instead.

## THURSDAY 3RD JULY

Cava-Sue is proper stressed right now 'cos her Theatre Studies A-Level group are putting on a play called *Waiting For Godot* by this bloke called Samuel Beckett and she has a lead role. I asked her what *Waiting For Godot* was about and she said, 'Well, on one level, Shiz, it's about two tramps waiting for their mate, Godot, to arrive, but on a deeper level it symbolizes lots of things like war and stilted ambition or the futility of modern existence.' Oh my days. It sounds more depressing than Christmas *EastEnders*. Why are all clever books miserable?

I told Cava-Sue about the two A– marks I got for English recently. Cava-Sue was really chuffed for me. She grabbed me and kissed my face! Cava-Sue said I've always had a brilliant imagination. Cava-Sue said, 'Hey Shiz, do you remember the time when you were three and you took the top off my Barbie dolls' house and did a poo in the bathroom area then told everyone that the jolly green giant did it?!' WHY DOES EVERYONE IN THIS FAMILY HAVE TO REMEMBER EVERY BLOODY THING?

## SATURDAY 5TH JULY

BIG NEWS. The G-Mayes Detonators have SPLIT UP due to musical differences!! Carrie says that Wesley completely refuses to add human beatbox on Bezzie's track, 'Girl, U Iz My Baby-Boo'. Carrie says that Bezzie is going to be a solo artist now and is working on a concept album devoted to songs mainly about his relationship with Carrie. Carrie says she's sending me an MP3 over of one called 'Clinton – Don't Diss My Wifey' that is so sweet that it made her cry.

It's like talking to someone with brain damage.

## WEDNESDAY 9TH JULY

Mum RSVPed the invite to Maria Draper, saying that we will all be attending the Draper Hydration Summer Barbecue. Mum seems quite excited by it. She can't wait to get a good nose round Draperville. She's not seen the hallway ceiling that Maria got painted like the Sistine Chapel in the Vatican, except all the angels have Maria's and Barney's and Carrie's faces on them. Maria is right proud of it. Maria rang up *Elle Decoration* and *Stylish Homes* magazines and asked if they wanted to take photos of it but they both said it was 'not really their type of thing'. I don't know how they can say that. The drawing of Alexis the Chihuahua with wings playing a lute is really tasteful. If that's not style, what is?

## FRIDAY 11TH JULY

Nan rang tonight and asked Mum to get her a ticket for Cava-Sue's play.

'Ooh! Is Cava-Sue in a play?' Mum said loudly. 'She never said!!' Cava-Sue looked up from her *Waiting For Godot* book and made a face like you would when your thong gets stuck up your bum-crack.

'Ooh it's ages since I've been to the theatre!' Mum said. ''Ere, Brian, when was the last time I saw a show?'

'We went to Goodmayes Social last year to see Jimmy Sparkle the Ventriloquist and his Cheeky Monkey, Rumpo,' Dad said.

'Ooh yeah!' laughed Mum. 'He was a right laugh! Will it be anything like that, Cava-Sue?'

'Not really,' said Cava-Sue, then she made the thong/bum-crack face again.

Mum is making Cava-Sue get three tickets for me, her and Gran. Cava-Sue looked very sad when I told her.

## WEDNESDAY 16TH JULY

Tonight me, Mum and Nan went to Cava-Sue's college to see *Waiting For Godot*. We nearly missed the start 'cos Mum was trying to set Sky+ for *Dog Borstal* and find her spare packet of Kensitas Club. Then Nan turned up dead late too 'cos she'd been at her Wednesday club and the meat raffle was late. By the time we got to the college we were last. We sat near the back like Cava-Sue told us to. She said that was where we'd get the best view. The audience was full of dead student sorts wearing weird hats and leg warmers and pixie shoes. Whenever I see Cava-Sue's mates these days they remind me of that game me and Carrie used to play at birthday parties in Year Seven where you put on tons of coats and hats and scarves and then spin round proper quick and have to eat a Mars Bar with a knife and fork. Their clothes never match and they always look a bit confused.

Eventually the lights went off and the curtain went up. Our Cava-Sue was standing on stage with another girl, both dressed as a tramps with mud smears on their faces! Me and Mum laughed out proper loud and cheered, but no one else did. Cava-Sue paced about a bit, then her and the other girl began talking and shouting words. I listened as hard as I could but I couldn't understand.

''Ere, Shiraz! What's she saying?' Mum said, nudging me. Nan started fiddling with her hearing aid. It began to squeak.

'Is it English?' Nan said. 'Is that our Cava-Sue?'

'Shhhhh!' said a woman in front, wearing thick-rimmed glasses.

'Shhhh yersel'!' said Mum. The woman tutted. ''Ere at least Cava-Sue's smartened herself up a bit!' Mum whispered at top volume.

The next half hour seemed to last FOR EVER. I thought the play might get better when more actors

146

joined in, but there WAS NO OTHER ACTORS aside from a weird-looking bloke who ran on now and then talking even more gibberish. Dunno whether he was even in the play or he just had learning difficulties and was lost. Then Mum's mobile phone rang, which was totally embarrassing, 'cos her ringtone is still 'In Da Club' by 50 Cent which me and Murphy put on her mobile three years ago for a joke. Everyone looked around and stared.

'Helloooo? Glo?' my mum said. 'All right darling? I can't talk. I'm in the theatre. IN THE THEATRE! Our Cava-Sue's in a play. Yeah. YEAH! I know! Nah, not really. Nah, it's not up to much. I ain't got a clue what's happening. It's in Cantonese I reckon!'

By this point people were beginning to tell Mum to shut up. Even Cava-Sue was getting distracted.

'So you got time to cut my Brian's hair or not then?' my mum said.

'Excuse me!' shouted the woman with the glasses. 'There is a no-mobile-phone rule during performances!'

'Oh Glo, I'll ring ya back. Some woman 'ere is taking the right hump,' sighed my mum.

'I am not some woman!' tutted the woman. 'I am Cava-Sue's drama teacher! I produced this performance.'

I looked up at the stage and Cava-Sue was staring down at us in the audience. She looked like she was going to explode.

Soon after that the lights went on and my mum stretched and yawned and said, ''Ere Shiraz, thank god that's over. My bum's gone dead!'

Then the announcer said, 'The interval will last fifteen minutes. Please return to your seats in good time for part two.'

'Part bloody two!' gasped my mum, then she woke Nan up and we went to Wetherspoon's over the road instead and had some buffalo wings and waited for Cava-Sue to come out.

Cava-Sue never said a single word all the way home.

Sometimes I think Cava-Sue is embarrassed about us.

## THURSDAY 17TH JULY

Ms Bracket cornered me today and asked me why my mum wasn't at Parents' Evening on Monday night. I said she was at work. This wasn't true. I didn't tell my mother there was a Parents' Evening on Monday night. She always makes a big deal about finishing work early to go, then there's always at least one teacher who bends her ear, then I get loads of earache at home just 'cos she got a load of earache at school. What's the point?

'Look Shiraz,' Ms Bracket said. 'Next year is crucial to you if you're going to get those GCSEs and stay on in sixth form. Your Geography and RE teacher and I know you are more than capable. Personally, I need to know you're getting support at home. Will you get your mum to come in and see me next term?'

She walked off leaving me in the corridor feeling a bit

stunned. Ms Bracket really DOES believe I can do A-Levels. I suppose if I'm real to myself, I do too.

## FRIDAY 18TH JULY

END OF TERM. Six whole weeks off! Walked home with Kezia and Luther covered in egg and felt-tip pen and Rice Krispies. Superchav Academy made the local news again. That 999 fire engine prank-call is becoming a bit of an Uma Brunton-Fletcher tradition. She's on the Ilford Fire Department central database of offenders now too. Uma is moving to Portsmouth for the summer to live with her real dad. Uma says this place is a shit-hole and she's probably never coming back. Carrie got picked up by Bezzie and they went off to sort out the decks for Sunday's Draper Hydration Summer Barbecue. She's hardly even mentioned me coming at all.

## SUNDAY 20TH JULY

It's 10pm. Even though I'm well tired I want to write down everything that happened as it might make me understand it more. Today was the Draper Hydration Summer Barbecue. My mum was up at 8am moaning at my dad to polish his shoes and find his tie, and standing beside mine and Cava-Sue's bunk beds yelling that it was a beautiful day and we should both put on our matching pink tracksuits and scrunchies and gold charm bracelets that she bought us from Granda's will money as we all had to look 'nice'. Mum is dead paranoid that Maria Draper thinks she's better than us just 'cos she's got more money. 'At least I make an honest living!' Mum kept saying. 'I didn't just stand flapping my eyelashes at blokes with money who came in the social club!'

Mum then went on to announce that in the 1980s Barney Draper had the 'glad eye' for her but she chose our dad instead. Dad groaned then and said that's why Barney Draper always smiles and toots his horn when he passes him in his van, 'cos he had a lucky bloody escape. Then Mum told Dad to shut up and have a shave and do something with his hair 'cos Aunty Glo had cut it far too short and he looked a bit like Hitler. Then I put on my bright pink H&M tracksuit and my white Adidas trainers and some foundation and a load of bronzer and my thickest gold hoops. Then Cava-Sue came down looking like a homeless as usual in her footless tights and frilly skirt and a T-shirt that said *Young and Lost*, and then Mum shouted at her and then she shouted back and then we all shouted at each other and eventually we left the house.

We got to Draperville and it was like the bloody Brit Awards. They had security guys on the gate with headsets checking invites and helping people park cars. When we got inside there were guests everywhere; all the Draper Hydration employees, all their families, Lewis, Kezia, their mums and dads and tons of the locals from the

Goodmayes Social Club. Collette Brown and her new boyfriend, Curtis, were there. Collette had a green bikini top and a sarong and big pair of dark glasses on and she looked well flash, like Victoria Beckham. Of course my mother had to show me up by shouting, ''Ere Collette, love that bikini, is it George at Asda?' and Collette just laughed and said 'Gucci'. Collette and my sister barely spoke. Cava-Sue hid inside most of the time moaning about getting skin cancer. The sun was really hot and everyone was drinking glasses of this stuff called Pimms with strawberry and cucumber floating in it, and fancy cocktails with fresh raspberries. At the side of the garden some blokes in white suits were playing 'When the Saints Go Marching In' on trombones and trumpets, and this circus clown was going around making balloons into sausage dogs. A whole pig was roasting on a spit and there were three grills covered in burgers and sausages. There were at least five whirlpool jacuzzi baths situated around the side of the garden too! My mother's eyes were bulging out of her head, then she whispered to me, ''Ere, this is a bit tacky isn't it? I dunno what they're trying to prove, we all know they've got more money than sense!' I texted Carrie to tell her I was here, but she didn't text back, so I decided to get some food.

And that's when I saw him. Wesley Barrington Bains II.

He was sitting on a little bench beside the koi carp pond, all by himself, texting someone. He had a pair of navy-blue jeans and white trainers on and a baseball cap and a thick gold chain over his Hackett polo shirt. He looked lovely. Really bloody lovely. I wanted to run right up and say hello but I didn't, I acted cool and I walked over slowly and said, 'All right, Billy-no-mates.'

He looked up with his totally lush green eyes and he said, 'Shiraz! All right babe?' then he stood up and gave me a little kiss on the face. 'Had any mashed rat dramas lately, innit?' he said.

'Nah mate, I am totally mashed rat free,' I said, and then we both laughed about me running down the road in the wellies.

'I was so like a knight in shining armour, innit?' Wesley said, proudly.

'Yeah you were!' I said. Just then some of the grown-ups started stripping their clothes off down to their swimming costumes and began getting into the whirlpools, which was so gross that me and Wesley could hardly talk for laughing. One geezer had a belly so big he looked like he was about to give birth to a hippo. Then, just as I was about to sit down and have a proper chat I heard Carrie's voice.

'Wesley? Wesley!? Has Bezzie found that spare lead yet?' said Carrie. 'I told him to do it for 3pm!' Carrie looked stunning. She was wearing a short navy-blue dress. Not her tracksuit or jeans. And she was wearing a TIARA! She had borrowed Collette Brown's tiara! She looked totally beautiful. Like a WAG. She saw me and grabbed me for a hug, shouting, 'Ooh! Shizza! You're here! I didn't know you were here! We were up in my bedroom putting on some more makeup!'

I looked over Carrie's shoulder and there was a girl standing there with straight blonde hair in a low-cut white dress. Her knockers were already sunburned.

'Shiraz,' said Carrie, 'this is Dee-Dee! You've never met each other before?'

'Hi,' said Dee-Dee, glaring at me.

'Dee-Dee,' said Wesley, 'this is the girl who I found outside the factory.'

It didn't sound as nice when he put it like that.

'Yeah, I know who Shiraz is,' said Dee-Dee, staring right at me.

We all stood about for a bit awkwardly, then Bezzie pitched up wearing a full Burberry tracksuit, holding some electrical leads, saying, 'Right peoples, now we can get dis bashment jumpin big-time!' He says stuff like that a lot. You get used to it after a while.

We all walked through the crowds together to the sun patio where Bezzie's decks were. Dee-Dee was whispering in Carrie's ear and linking Wesley's arms and they were all saying something about a car cruise they'd all gone to recently. I started to feel really angry then. Especially as it then dawned on me that when Bezzie said he was going to play 'some tunes', he actually meant 'his own tunes', meaning for the next hour he was dropping stuff like 'Girl U Iz My Baby-Boo' and 'Clinton – Don't Diss My Wifey' which he then MC'D OVER HIMSELF. And he sounded rubbish. It sounded like a drunk person arguing with a dustbin but Carrie and Dee-Dee thought it was AMAZING. All the grown-ups seemed to think it was funny and they started dancing around and at one point I looked over and to my bloody horror my mum and dad, who looked well hammered, were doing fake hip-hop dancing. God, I could have died. Carrie, Bezzie and Dee-Dee were laughing and cheering them on. Wesley gave me a look like he could see I was embarrassed.

'Woo-hoo!' laughed Dee-Dee. 'Shake that ass!' Then Dee-Dee started doing an impersonation of my mother and everyone was laughing more.

Something inside me just snapped. I stormed off upstairs to the loo with Carrie following after me. She pushed her arm through mine and pulled me back.

'Shiz, what's up?' she said. I just tutted and said I was OK.

'Come on Shiz, tell me what's up!' she said, sounding like she actually cared. What a faker. I just decided to totally tell her the truth.

'Oh you wanna know what's wrong, do you?!' I said. 'Bloody Dee-Dee. That's what's up.'

'What about Dee-Dee?' she said.

'What's she doing here? Snotty cow,' I said.

Carrie looked stunned. 'I had to invite her, Shiz. She's Wesley's bird. And she's my mate now too.'

My face flushed red then. 'Yeah, too right, I know that! That's why I never see you any more! That's why we never hang out no more! 'Cos when you're not with bloody Bezzie, you're with Dee-Dee! You treat me like crap these days.'

'No I don't!' said Carrie, but she looked a bit guilty.

'You only see me when there's no one else! I only found out about this barbecue 'cos my mum was invited! You've changed! The moment you met Bezzie Kelleher you changed!'

Carrie's lip wobbled. Good, I thought, I hope she cries.

'That's not true!' she said.

'Yes it is! You're totally not the same person now you're with Bezzie,' I shouted. 'You even kicked me out of the car on the street! You're an airhead and a user! And by the way, your Bezzie can't rap! And he's not even buff or nothing – he's MINGING!'

Carrie's mouth fell open then.

'And I hope you're all happy together,' I shouted. 'You and munter and Wesley and sunburned knockers. Have a nice life. Laterz!'

I turned around and stormed off down the stairs, but then Carrie shouted after me, 'Oh well, suit yourself Shiraz, you mardy cow! Don't take it out on me 'cos you fancy Wesley Barrington Bains II and he don't fancy you back. Which he don't by the way! He loves Dee-Dee! You blew that one being your usual awkward-cow self!' Carrie's voice started to crack a bit then. 'And don't diss my Bezzie 'cos I love him and we're going to be together for ever! And, er, that's how it is! Build a bridge and get over it, you silly mare!'

I turned round to shout something back but Carrie was really crying then. And by the time I got to the garden gate I was too.

# AUGUST

## FRIDAY 1ST AUGUST

I am so totally not speaking to Carrie Draper. And I so DON'T CARE. If she wants to spend the school holiday with stupid Dee-Dee, munter Bezzie and Mr Smooth Wesley in their stupid cars going to stupid car cruises then that suits me fine. How anyone manages to fit in a car with Dee-Dee and those monstrous melons is a bleeding miracle anyhow. Good riddance to all of them. I am really happy. I'm keeping it real.

## SUNDAY 3RD AUGUST

Still not speaking to Carrie. I don't miss her at all. Got better stuff to do this summer like watching telly, sunbathing and being personal trainer to the dog. Penny needs to lose weight. The vet says that unless she does more exercise and stops eating Ginsters pasties she will die. I don't want Penny to die, she has been very supportive during my fall-out with Carrie. I took Penny to Goodmayes Park this afternoon for a run. She frolicked like a normal dog for a bit then she smelled a burger van and lay down sulking until I bought her a hot-dog. Not everyone can be as positive and motivated as me.

## WEDNESDAY 6TH AUGUST

Poor Penny. I just measured her out 200g of Purina Lo-fat Science Diet from the vet. She stared at it, looking proper depressed. It's for her own good. Just like when I told Carrie that Bezzie was a minger who couldn't rap. It was for her own good!

I feel well bad about that now. Not that I think about Carrie Draper much. Well, OK, I did just then, but that was the first time today, right?

## FRIDAY 8TH AUGUST

Mum came home from work today in a right mood. Me, Murphy and Cava-Sue were all lying about bored on the settee eating Pringles watching CITV when Murphy shouts at Mum, 'Oi! What'ya making for tea?' For some reason this sent Mum loopy.

'What am I making for tea?' Mum shouted. 'What are YOU lot making ME for tea? You're as fit as I am!' We all stared at her 'cos she was obviously having some sort of mentalist episode. 'Look at you all!' she yelled. 'You lazy bloody lumps! Do you think I'm a slave? Is this what you think you're doing for the summer holidays? Dossing about on your fat behinds eating crisps?' I informed Mum that I wasn't dossing, I was supervising the dog's weight-loss regime. 'Well you're doing a blindin' job there Shiraz,' shouted Mum, ''cos the front door was left open and I just found her down at Aunty Glo's house eating jam tarts!'

## SATURDAY 9TH AUGUST

Mum has made a home-duties chart. She saw it on this show called *The Terrible Teen Tamer* on ITV. She's put a chart in the kitchen and some stickers and some felt-tip pens and when we do our housework chore we've got to mark it off on the chart and get a gold star. If we get three gold stars we get an extra £2 a week allowance. According to *The Terrible Teen Tamer* this will make everyone stop wanting to kill each other.

Cava-Sue started whining right away 'cos she has to clean the bathroom. Cava-Sue says Murphy's bumhole is a law unto itself and he can clean up his own skidmarks. Then Mum got narky and said HARD LUCK 'cos she's been in charge of EVERYBODY'S bloody skidmarks for the last twenty years and she wants a day off. Then Cava-Sue got upset and shouted that 'this entire family has a conspiracy to break her spirit'. Then Murphy chipped in that there was NO WAY he was hanging out the washing as it was a girl's job and he wasn't touching anyone's thongs. So I said I'd swap with Murphy and he could do the dusting and polishing instead. Then Cava-Sue said that was TOTALLY UNFAIR 'cos that meant Murphy had the easiest job as usual. So Mum told Cava-Sue to shut up 'cos Murphy is a boy and he's no good at housework.

Then Cava-Sue got really angry at Mum and said that maybe if Mum hadn't been such a bloody dinosaur in her attitudes and made Dad and Muphy do some housework then they'd be less helpless and Mum wouldn't be such a slave in the first place. Mum told her to shut up and go and wash her hair 'cos it was greasy. 'It's like living in the Dark Ages before feminism happened!' squealed Cava-Sue, storming off.

'Well if you don't like it here then you know where the door is!' shouted Mum.

I went to my room sharpish before I ended up on skidmark patrol.

## SUNDAY 10TH AUGUST

No one has got a gold star yet. I put the dog on the bathroom scales. She has put on two kilos. I am trying to stay positive but it is quite hard. I looked at Carrie's Bebo site for ages today. She has gone to the Dominican Republic for three weeks with her mum and dad. Carrie's family always have dead good holidays. They actually enjoy spending time together. They never chuck felt-tips at each other's heads or draw rude pictures of each other with willies poking out their heads on home-duties charts. I miss going to Draperville.

## TUESDAY 12TH AUGUST

Cava-Sue says she will NOT co-operate with the rota any more as the gold star scheme is completely UNJUST. Why should Murphy get a star for playing Zombie Armageddon in his underpants with a can of Mr Sheen polish sitting next to him? Mum said, 'Fair enough, but I'm NOT lending you another penny and you can stop farting about with that drama course and get a job right now!'

Cava-Sue went mental then and shouted, 'You never wanted me to get an education anyway so that'll suit you just fine. That's why you came up the college making a big show of me during my play!'

So Mum shouted, 'I think you were making a big enough display of yourself, Cava-Sue! And I don't care what you do as long as you bring some money into the house and stop scrounging.'

Then Cava-Sue shouted that she wasn't a scrounger and the only reason she'd asked to lend £20 yesterday was 'cos her student overdraft hadn't cleared and she was going to The Secret Underground festival that weekend with Lewis.

Then Mum laughed and said that there was NO WAY Cava-Sue was going to the Magic Underpant festival or whatever it was called with all her soap-dodger mates 'cos Mum's changed her mind about the loan now 'cos of all Cava-Sue's lip.

Cava-Sue looked totally furious then. She slammed down her copy of *NME* magazine and stormed upstairs. There was a lot of banging, then she came down carrying a big holdall and three plastic carrier bags and a sleeping bag and some files. She looked at Mum and shouted, 'I hope you're happy now, you bloody witch! I never want to see you again!' and walked out slamming the door.

Mum put down her cup of tea and went to the window and watched her storming off up Thundersley Road. Mum's hands were shaking and she looked like she was about to cry, but she didn't stop Cava-Sue going.

## THURSDAY 14TH AUGUST

Cava-Sue has not come home for two days. She's ignoring my texts. I know she's probably just at Lewis's house sulking or something. She'll come home. It's quite good having the bedroom to myself. I can listen to whatever music I like and have the light on as late as I want. I brought the portable TV from the kitchen upstairs last night and watched *Hollyoaks* in bed. It was weird not having Cava-Sue slagging it off all the time for being 'poorly structured'.

## SUNDAY 17TH AUGUST

Still no word from Cava-Sue. I texted her a few times today but she never texted back. Then I rang her phone and it went to voicemail. I don't know how Cava-Sue will pay for any top-up credits on her mobile as she has no money. I wish she would call me. I have moved into her top bunk. Penny has the bottom one. It is much comfier up here but it doesn't quite feel right as I never sleep this high. I wonder how Cava-Sue is coping with sleeping so low?

## TUESDAY 19TH AUGUST

THIS HOUSE IS DOING MY HEAD IN. Today I asked where everyone reckons Cava-Sue is. Dad just made one of his 'don't start trouble' faces and Murphy just pretended to be deaf. My mum just lit up a fag and picked up the *Sun*.

'Are you not bothered where she is!? It's been a week!' I said to Mum.

'She's the one who left,' muttered my mum from behind her paper. 'I've devoted my whole life to doing my best for that girl and all she does is throw it back in my face. When she wants to apologize to me she can. I certainly won't be.'

Cava-Sue will NEVER apologize. Once, when we were little, Cava-Sue pushed a yellow crayon right up my nose and it got stuck. She never said sorry. Even when we got to the hospital all she did was ask the nurse for the crayon back 'cos she'd not finished colouring in her rainbow.

I hate these summer holidays. It's crap without Carrie and Cava-Sue. Got the bus to Nan's house. She made me a pork chop and some mashed potato and a glass of Vimto. Then I sat on Granda's old chair and we ate Fox's Glacier Mints and played Beggar My Neighbour, which is a card game only me and her seem to know. I told Nan I was quite depressed 'cos I've fell out with Carrie and Cava-Sue has going missing. Nan sat quiet for a bit. She said she could help with one bit. Nan said she knew where Cava-Sue was. Nan says she's been trying not to get involved 'cos my mum already says she's an interfering old bag. Nan says that Cava-Sue is in London. I felt sick when she said that, imagining Cava-Sue sitting at a cashpoint with a scabby face and a begging cup, being a homeless. Nan says it's not as bad as it sounds. Nan says Cava-Sue and Lewis are staying at a friend's in Kentish Town in north-west London. A FRIEND CALLED PIXIE!!!? Nan says Cava-Sue came to her house last week and was upset and says she hates Mum and she's never coming back to Goodmayes ever, but Nan reckons it might all blow over. Nan lent Cava-Sue £100 so she's not broke.

I stared out of the window all the way home on the bus and thought about Cava-Sue. I miss her loads. I wish there was something I could do. What do I do?

Carrie would know what to do. 'She who dares wins,

Shiraz,' that's what she'd say. Carrie was the one with all the good ideas.

## TUESDAY 26TH AUGUST

Cava-Sue has been gone two weeks. I lay in bed most of today with the dog, reading *Heat* magazine and the last chapters of *Jane Eyre* again. I like the bit at the end when Jane Eyre gets together with that Mr Rochester geezer who she fancies and they live happily ever after. Jane Eyre had a right old crap life up until then 'cos she's small and unlucky and plug-ugly too, just like me. It's nice to think that there is love out there for people like me and not just Carrie and Collette Brown.

I told Mum today that Cava-Sue is in London and Mum should bloody do something about it. Mum said I should go and bloody join her then she can turn our room into a solarium.

Mum is only pretending to be not bothered. At night I sometimes hear her downstairs crying.

## SUNDAY 31ST AUGUST

Something PROPER STRANGE happened today. I was sitting in my bedroom listening to the Radio One Dave Pearce's Sunday Night Soundclash Bender and sharing a packet of Penguins with Penny (who has fallen off her diet big style) when Mum shouted up the stairs that I had a visitor. I looked out of the window and I nearly died. Standing by our garden gate was Wesley Barrington Bains II! He spotted me looking down at him and smiled. I put some lipgloss on and my gold hoops and stuck some chewing gum in my gob and went downstairs.

'All right Wesley,' I said, like it was totally normal he was at my front door.

'Y'all right Shiraz? Nice day, innit?' he said.

''Spose,' I said. We stood and stared at each other for a bit.

I love you, I thought.

'Got a favour to ask,' he said.

'Go on,' I said.

He took me over to the boot of the banana-yellow Golf and flipped it open. In the boot was a bin bag.

'Will you be seeing Carrie at school next week?' he said, looking a bit awkward.

'Well, she's in my class,' I said. 'Suppose so.'

'Can you give her this?' Wesley said. 'It's all her stuff that she left round at Bezzie's house, innit. Presents and clothes and stuff.'

'What?' I said.

'He's dumped her, innit?' said Wesley. 'Bezzie wants me to go over and chuck it all over the fence at Draperville, but I don't wanna.'

Poor Carrie! She must be bleeding devastated, I thought.

'What's he dumped her for?' I said.

''Cos Carrie got back from Dominican yesterday with a big love bite on her neck,' said Wesley. 'Then Bezzie found this picture on her phone of her sitting on the knee of this big bloke with dreads called Raphael who did the boat trips, innit.'

My mouth fell open. Carrie!

'What's Bezzie sayin'?' I said.

'He says she's a skank and a ho and she's dumped, innit,' said Wesley.

For some reason that made me quite mad. Bezzie might have got it all wrong. I didn't like him dissing Carrie.

'Well why don't Bezzie go throw the stuff over the fence at Draperville himself if he's such a big man?' I said, folding my arms and doing that rudegirl head wobble that Uma's dead good at.

'He would,' said Wesley, 'but he's too busy rewriting all of the lyrics to his concept album, innit.'

We both looked at each other. Then Wesley smiled and I couldn't help myself a little bit too.

I looked at the bag again and rolled my eyes at him.

'All right,' I said, 'I'll take it for her.'

'Awwww thanks Shiz, you're an angel,' Wesley smiled, looking dead relieved. 'Look I owe you one, innit? If I can do anything for you at any time. Just give me a call.'

'Whatever,' I said.

'Honestly, Shiz, anything,' he shouted.

I took the bag and walked back into the house and

didn't bother with any more small talk, 'cos I'm sure he needed to be somewhere. Like with bloody Dee-Dee.

# SEPTEMBER

## TUESDAY 2ND SEPTEMBER

Back to school for the first day of Year Eleven.

I got up this morning at 7am and I ironed my school uniform and packed my new pens into my new pencil case and packed the bag of Carrie's stuff into a posher plastic bag and walked to school with Uma Brunton-Fletcher. Uma's been in Portsmouth for the summer, living with her real dad and his new girlfriend, Mica. Uma was going to stay there for good but it didn't work out. Uma says she's not bothered or nothing. Uma says her dad's girlfriend Mica is only five years older than her so she's not acting like her bloody mother when she's not even her real mother. Uma says Mica is a slut and she needs a proper slap. We walked up the driveway to Mayflower and there were cement mixers and scaffolding poles everywhere and a load of blokes building a new extension where the overflow car park used to be.

''Ere, bruv, what's happening?' shouted Uma at one of the builders.

'It's the new sixth-form block, sweetheart,' said this bloke in an orange jacket and a hard hat.

Uma just tutted. 'Oh right, it'd have to be something for the freaks and swots, wouldn't it, Shiz?'

'Mmm . . . Yeah,' I said.

'They get everything in this world,' sneered Uma, then she flicked her fag end into the rubble and stormed off. I stood and looked at the block for a minute and felt a bit excited.

Carrie wasn't at school today. Maria sent a message saying she's ill. I had a whole speech planned out to smooth over all the grief what's happened and then she didn't even show up.

## WEDNESDAY 3RD SEPTEMBER

Carrie came to school today. I didn't get to say any of my speech. It all went arse up. I walked into Tutor Group and there she was at the back with Uma and Chantalle and Kezia. At first I thought she was proper ill or something 'cos she was so pale, then I realized it was the first time since June I'd seen her without her Onyx spray tan. Carrie was clutching a pile of tissues and her eyes were proper red. She looked at me pathetically and then looked away. Chantalle had her arm round her shoulder saying stuff like, 'They're all bastards Carrie, that's what my mother said when she got divorced the second time!' Kezia was telling a story about some geezer who got her sister knocked up then it turned out he had another wife and kids in Leytonstone. Uma grabbed the arm of my pink trackie top and pulled me away.

'Carrie's Bezzie has dumped her!' she said, like it was suddenly all Uma's business.

'I know,' I said, quite grumpy like.

'She says her life ain't worth living no more,' said Uma.

'Oh,' I said.

The bell went soon after and we all walked out to the lockers.

''Ere, Carrie, wait on,' I said as she passed me. Carrie stopped. She looked proper small and thin like she'd been on one of her silly celery-only diets again.

'What?' she said.

'I'm, like, well sorry about you and Bezzie,' I said. I totally meant it but even I knew how fake it sounded. Last time I spoke to Carrie I said he was well butterz and a knobhead or something equally shady.

'Thanks . . .' said Carrie, then her lip started to wobble.

'I got something for you,' I said. 'I got something from Bezzie.'

'What?' she said. 'What is it?' Carrie's face suddenly looked really hopeful. What a mess I was making of this.

'Hang on,' I said, then I opened my locker and brought out the plastic bag. Carrie opened it and peered inside. She put her hand in and brought out a small plastic frog with its foot smashed off. She stared at it, then she stared at me.

'Where d'you get this?!' she said.

'Wesley brought it to my house,' I said.

'He brought it to your house!?' Carrie said, staring at the frog. 'Why? What's this got to do with you and Wesley?!'

Carrie was getting all up in my face now, proper mad and that. I chucked my shoulders back to front her out.

''Ere don't you get the hump with me!' I said. 'Bezzie wanted Wesley to chuck all your stuff over the fence at Draperville. I stopped him.'

Carrie opened her mouth, then closed it again.

'Oh I bet you're loving this, aren't you?' she said.

'No I'm not,' I said, totally straight up 'cos honestly I am totally NOT.

'Yeah you are. You always hated Bezzie and now we've split up,' Carrie shouted.

'Well if you've split up it's not my fault!' I shouted back. 'You're the one who got off with the guy who did the bloody boat trips.'

Carrie looked proper outraged then.

'Who told you that?!' she fumed.

'Everyone knows that!' I said.

'That's not even true!' she snapped. 'I didn't bloody get off with anyone! It wasn't a love bite, it was a bleeding mosquito bite. I only sat on that bloke's knee for ten seconds. Why does no one believe me?'

I looked at her and felt proper bad then.

'I believe you,' I said, but she wasn't listening at all now.

Carrie threw the bag into her locker and slammed the door.

'It's a good job your life is so bloody perfect, isn't it?' sobbed Carrie, then she walked off blowing her nose. I wanted to shout after her that my life wasn't perfect at all. That I had lost my best friend and Cava-Sue had moved out and I was proper lonely and I wanted everything back to normal, that I was sorry about everything. But I ain't bloody apologizing to her. Us Wood women never do.

## FRIDAY 5TH SEPTEMBER

Uma Brunton-Fletcher has told Kezia and Chantalle that I am somehow to blame for Carrie and Bezzie splitting up. They were all sitting on the back row of Tutor Group today being all off with me, so I just did a whatever face at them, got my stuff and moved to another desk. In Religious Studies today we were learning about the Muslim celebration of Eid. We were using this bleeding boring old text book with pictures of folk praying, so I told everyone about Tariq's big brother's Eid firework party with the good buffet that Murphy goes to. This made everyone who wasn't Muslim understand it all a bit better. Mrs Radowitz was well pleased with me. This made Uma and Kezia even more moody 'cos I was being a 'Kiss-ass'. I reckon I could pass GCSE Religion as well as English. I'm going to have a shot at Geography and Maths too. I wish I could tell Cava-Sue.

## SUNDAY 7TH SEPTEMBER

I went to Nan's for Sunday dinner today. When I got there she'd turned her hearing aid off by mistake and she couldn't hear the phone so I had to bang on the door like a proper nutjob for ages. All the neighbours came out and stared at me like I was a criminal. I wanted to scream, 'It's only a flaming pink hoodie! I'm not breaking in to nick anyone's pension book! Hoodies have nans too, y'know, you predjudicial bloody stigmatizing weirdos!'

Nan had done a roast leg of lamb with some roast potatoes and mint sauce and gravy. I ate it in about five gulps without even breathing 'cos it was so gorgeous and the food is crap at my house at the moment. Even crapper than it normally is.

I told Gran that my mum has stopped cooking tea. Mum says she's fed up being 'everyone's bleeding gopher'. Mum says we can all help our bleeding selves. I told Nan how Mum comes in from work and changes into a big cardigan and trackie pants and watches her Sky+ recording of *Fast-Track Family Feud* on ITV2 and smokes fags and doesn't want to laugh about anything. I think she's depressed about Cava-Sue.

'Mother,' I shouted at her the other day, 'Cava-Sue, my big sister and your daughter, is sharing a room in a flat in Kentish Town with a girl called Pixie and they've been busking for money. IN CASE YOU CARE.'

My mum just looked at me. She pressed pause on the Sky+.

'Does she want to come home?' Mum said.

'I don't know. I don't know nothing else,' I said, even though I knew that was a double negative and Ms Bracket would've red pen circled it. My mum looked at me then she looked back at *Fast-Track Family Feud* again.

'That's the problem with Cava-Sue,' said Mum blankly. 'There ain't no magic wands for folk like her. She's got to want to change. She needs to give me some respect. She don't give me no respect. I always gave my mother respect. I didn't agree with my mother's ideas but I gave her proper respect.'

My mum pushed play on the TV show where two brothers who both got the same girl pregnant were having a big fight. Reuben Smart, *Fast-Track Family Feud*'s presenter, sent them both backstage to speak to someone called 'Kirsten, who is trained'. I wish Kirsten-who-is-trained would talk to my mum and Cava-Sue.

'They need their heads banged together,' said Nan, when I told her all of this. Then we both had some apple crumble.

## FRIDAY 12TH SEPTEMBER

In lunch today I hid in the computer lab at school 'cos me trying harder in lessons is going down proper badly with

Uma, Kezia and Luther. I dunno what Carrie thinks. She's on another bloody planet. Her heart is totally broken. I logged on to my Bebo and there were no messages from anyone important. I looked at Cava-Sue's page again but it hasn't been updated for months. Neither had Lewis's either. Then I began clicking through Cava-Sue's friends' pages, not really concentrating or anything, and pretty soon I found PIXIE007. Pixie! Who my sister is living with!

Pixie is eighteen and she has black bobbed hair with blue streaks in the front and her photo is of her with a rose in her mouth holding a glass of red wine. Her page is full of arty drawings and poetry. She is obsessed with this old group called The Libertines. Her pictures are all of house parties full of people that look just like her and Cava-Sue. One photo – that I couldn't stop staring at – was of Pixie and Cava-Sue and Lewis in the living-room of a house and there was about three hundred people crammed in and a band playing in the middle and everyone was jumping up and down going mental. I looked at that for ages and felt a bit weird. Cava-Sue looked well happy. I looked through all of Pixie's Bebo comments. One comment from a girl called Esmerelda really caught my eye. It said this:

Hey Pix – Just got tickets for DIY Taxidermy at Milo on 20th!! See U and Cavasoo and Lewy down the front again!??

I typed 'DIY Taxidermy' into Google and found out that they are playing a nightclub called Milo on Oxford

St, London W1 on September twentieth.

I've got a plan, but I don't know if I dare do it.

## WEDNESDAY 17TH SEPTEMBER

Went to the computer lab again today at lunch. I'm getting less weird looks from all the computer nerds now. At first they thought I just wanted to thieve one of the laptops, 'cos in Year Nine, Uma once got caught down at Cash 4 Trash with one up her school jumper. 'I need to print out some street maps,' I told Sanjay Biswas from Year Nine, who was at the computer beside me.

'Use this site then,' he said, tapping out a web-address on the keyboard. 'Do you have the postcode of where you're going?' he said.

'Yeah,' I said. 'London W1.'

Sanjay helped me with the printer. I've got the maps now. All I need now is some transport.

## SATURDAY 20TH SEPTEMBER

I packed the maps and my lipgloss and my purse and my pink scrunchy and a spare neon-green scrunchy and an emergency packet of biscuits into my white H&M handbag. I ironed my pink hoodie, my navy Nike T-shirt, my fake Evisu jeans and put on my whitest Adidas trainers and my thick gold hoops. I looked in the mirror and thought about stuffing my bra with panty-pads 'cos my breasts still ain't made much of an appearance, but then I thought no, 'cos this is all about keeping it real. I told Mum I was off to play bingo in Chadwell Heath with Nan and left the house. At 6pm I stood outside The Spirit of Siam Chinese restaurant on the High Street and I felt proper scared. I couldn't decide whether what I was doing was well brave or proper thick but I'd started this now so I had to go through with it. All I wanted to do was see Cava-Sue and know she's all right and tell her she has to come home.

I started to think about Cava-Sue coming home and sleeping in the top bunk again and how this time I would stick up for her in front of Mum and say it was a good thing that she was doing an A-Level and that she wasn't a scrounger. I'd say that in fact Cava-Sue was an inspiration and that I wanted to do an A-Level too. Then I started to feel scared and think how much easier this would all be if Carrie was here with me 'cos she's good at planning things and persuading folk to do stuff. Then a car horn beeped and I looked up and it was him.

'Y'all right?' I said, getting into the banana-yellow Golf.

'Yeah,' he said. 'Sorry I'm late. Roads are all backed up in Ilford, innit.' He smelled of sports deodorant and chewing gum. 'You know where we're going?'

'Course I do,' I said.

'You sure, innit?' he laughed.

'I've got a map,' I said, waving some papers in his face. 'Come on, let's go.'

Me and Wesley set off to London, listening to Kiss FM and not talking much. I didn't know how much Wesley would want to know about what I wanted to do in central London 'cos he's a boy and most boys aren't that bothered about girls' feelings and emotions, and this is all about those type of things. I can't explain why I want to see Cava-Sue. It's all about emotions.

Anyway, soon Wesley asked me what was going on at home and I started to tell him all about the house-duties chart with the rude graffiti and Cava-Sue buying dresses off eBay and her refusing to clear up Murphy's skidmarks and our dog being on a diet but eating Aunty Glo's jam tarts and Cava-Sue kicking off about complex carbohydrate in her pizza and all that stuff. Wesley was really laughing at bits of it. Wesley said that my house sounded like it had plenty of banter going on. I thought about that for a second and suddenly felt a bit sad. We do have some proper barneys at Thundersley Road but we laugh a lot too. Like when Dad makes his cross-eyed face when Mum is telling a story. Or when me and Cava-Sue make dances up in the kitchen. Or when Mum's doing the ironing and she puts a pair of Dad's underpants on her head with a totally serious face and says, ''Ere, kids, I'm just off down the shops.' She's done that ever since we were little and it's still really funny.

'I wish my house was a bit noisier,' said Wesley. 'It's just me and Mum. I always wanted a brother or a sister. But

I've not got anyone. Well, I got Bezzie but he's not like my blood brother or nothing.'

We drove into the Wanstead tunnel.

I didn't know what to say for a bit, then I said, 'Do you remember your dad, what he was like and all that?'

'Just bits,' said Wesley. 'Just blurs and shapes and stuff really. He was really tall. Well he seemed tall to me. He smelled of oil 'cos he was always fixing his motor. He used to crawl about the carpet on all fours with me on his back laughing his head off.' Wesley stopped for a second then he thought really hard. 'I can remember a time at Christmas when we made a snowman on Goodmayes Park and he held me up in his arms to poke the carrot in for the nose . . . but that's about it, innit.'

I looked out of the window. We were coming into Leytonstone. I thought about how weird it must be to have no sister or brother or dad. I suddenly felt totally grateful for my lot.

'Thanks for driving me,' I said to Wesley.

'No worries,' he said. 'That's what friends are for, innit.'

We drove on for a few more miles through Hackney in east London. It was dark now and the traffic was busy and it started to feel more built up and scruffy and dirty, then we headed towards central London and I started to feel quite sick then as I totally didn't have a clue where we were and it was proper hectic with people everywhere. We parked at least a mile away from Oxford Street, then we walked the rest of the way through posh people going to the opera and smelly hot-dog stands and pigeons and poor people sleeping under newspapers and clubbers all dressed up to go clubbing and tourists wandering about with rucksacks and people going home from shopping in fancy boutiques. I stopped and looked at my notes again.

*Young and Lost club – every Saturday at Milo, 324 Oxford Street – doors open 9.30pm 20th September – DIY Taxidermy on stage 10.30pm*

Eventually we found the nightclub, Milo. It was 9.15pm. Wesley and me went into a McDonald's over the road and we bought a Big Tasty meal each and sat in the window. The doors weren't open at the club yet so a queue was beginning to form. The girls all looked a bit like Cava-Sue, all dressed in weird outfits like old-fashioned coats and high heels and pearl necklaces and weird berets, the boys looked like Lewis in skinny jeans and messy hair and baggy jumpers. I tried to eat my fries but I was proper nervous. The doors opened and people started to file in and my fries were going cold so Wesley ate them and I checked my print-out ten times to make sure I was at the right place. Then suddenly I spotted a group of people walking down the far side of the street, laughing and drinking cans of lager. My heart started to beat really really fast. I could see Cava-Sue!

She had a little white furry coat on and a green frilly skirt and high heels and a big black leather bag over her shoulder. She was swigging from a can of lager and her arm was linked through another girl's who looked like it might be Pixie. Pixie was wearing a green army jacket, baseball boots and a navy-blue T-shirt dress so short you could see her bum cheeks. I forgot all my plans to be cool then and ran out of McDonald's and ran over the road and jumped out in front of them both.

'Cava-Sue! Cava-Sue!' I said, looking right in her face. Her eye-makeup was thick and black like a witch. Cava-Sue looked at me, then her face lit up.

'Shiraz!' she shouted, then she grabbed me and gave me a big cuddle. 'Shiraz! What are you doing here? How? . . . Why? . . . Shiraz, does Mum know you're here?'

I stared at her and held on to her hands.

'Who's this, Cav?' said Pixie, staring at my hoops and hoodie, then at Wesley's gold chain and Hackett jumper like we were bloody martians or something.

'This is my little sister,' said Cava-Sue, who looked quite choked up now. 'This is Shiraz Bailey Wood!'

'Shiraz?' said Pixie. 'Like the red wine?'

'Like the red wine,' laughed Cava-Sue, then she gave me another hug. 'Shiraz, what are you doing here?'

'I've come to take you home,' I said. As soon as I said it, I realized how retarded it sounded. 'I want you to come home,' I said again, quieter this time.

'Oh . . . Shiz,' said Cava-Sue, 'I ain't coming home. I ain't coming home again ever.'

'But . . .' I began. 'Please! I won't borrow your stuff any more. And I'll do all your housework duties. And I'll stick up for you when Mum says you're a scrounger. Things would be different this time.'

Cava-Sue looked at me proper sadly.

'Oh Shiz, none of this is your fault,' she said, smoothing my hair down with her hand. 'You've not done anything wrong. This is between me and Mum.'

I looked at her and wanted to cry.

'Mum is upset y'know?' I told her. 'She's proper depressed.'

'Yeah, right,' said Cava-Sue, shaking her head. 'Mum doesn't care about me.'

'Yes she does,' I said.

'No she doesn't,' said Cava-Sue. 'Y'know what? Mum should adopt Collette bloody Brown to be her daughter, that's who she bloody loves. She always loved Collette. I'm a big bloody disappointment. But y'know what, Shiz? I can't be Collette Brown!'

Cava-Sue gave me another hug. Then she looked straight into my eyes.

'I ain't putting up with all her crap any more, Shiz!' she said. 'There's a world outside Goodmayes y'know? A world where you don't have to wear fake tan and get your nails done and go down Jumping Jacks of a Friday. You don't have to get pregnant by some random when you're twenty like everyone else, y'know?'

I stood there, proper still then. Not knowing what to say. Cava-Sue wrapped her fingers round mine.

'Y'know something, Shiz?' she said. 'I suddenly

realized that folk like me and you can do stuff with our lives. We can get a degree and get a good job and travel places and see the world, y'know?'

I nodded at her. Traffic was sweeping past us in the road, drowning her out, so she made her voice even louder.

'And we can wear whatever we want, y'know?' she said. 'We can say whatever we want and think whatever we want and do whatever we bloody want and live our lives however we want without someone – someone who's done NOTHING with their bloody life except stand in a betting shop – telling us what we can do with it.'

Cava-Sue stopped talking then. She shook her head and laughed at her own rant.

'But I miss you, Cava-Sue,' I said, quietly.

'I miss you too, Shiz,' she said, holding my hand. 'I miss all of you, proper bad. I even miss Mum. Despite the fact she's a total bloody bag.'

We stared at each other for a while. All of Cava-Sue's friends had gone into the club. Wesley was sitting on the step of Waterstone's book shop nearby, texting someone, or least pretending to.

'Go home, Shiz,' said Cava-Sue. Her eye-makeup was beginning to run.

She gave me another kiss, then she made Wesley promise to take me back to Goodmayes.

'Don't worry, Shizza,' Cava-Sue shouted as me and Wesley walked away. 'Things will work out.'

I wanted to believe her. But somehow I didn't.

The journey home seemed to take three times as long as on the way there.

## TUESDAY 23RD SEPTEMBER

I'm keeping my head down at school at the moment. Staying out of trouble. Uma's well glad that Carrie and me are hardly speaking 'cos she gets her all to herself. Uma and Carrie went to Ilford Mall together on Saturday.

'That was a proper laugh, wasn't it?' said Uma.

'Yeah,' said Carrie, although her face wasn't making her 'that was a proper laugh look' at all. Not like when we used to play That's Your Boyfriend together or eat ice cream with M&Ms or sing to her iPod on the rocking horses in the park.

That WAS a proper laugh.

Ms Bracket kept me behind after English today. She asked me if I'd thought any more about studying at Mayflower next year. I said I wanted to but it was complicated.

'How complicated?' she said.

'Too complicated for me to explain,' I said.

Ms Bracket raised her eyebrow and said, 'Shiraz Bailey Wood, with your vocabulary and intelligence, I very much doubt that.'

I pulled up a chair and began to talk. And talk. And talk. And by the time I'd finished talking I'd had another one of my brilliant ideas.

# OCTOBER

## WEDNESDAY 1ST OCTOBER

Shiraz Bailey Wood
34, Thundersley Road
Goodmayes
Essex
IG5 2XS
shirazbaileywood@hotmail.com

Dear Fast-Track Family Feud,

I am wondering if you could help me out with my family as they are jarring my head big style at the moment and you are quite possibly my last hope before I strangle the lot of them.

I watch your show most days on ITV2 and it seems like you can work miracles. I really enjoyed today's show, 'Mum, you're a drunk. Keep your junk in the trunk!' featuring the Jackson family from Scarborough who stopped speaking to their mum 'cos she was a right old alco who kept on flashing her bum and boobs in the local pub on karaoke night. One minute everyone was crying and threatening to get ASBOs on each other, then ten minutes spent backstage with Kirsten-who-is-trained and they were all happy again and talking about going to Falaraki next summer. I wish you could do that for my family too.

My name is Shiraz Bailey Wood. I'm nearly sixteen and I live in Essex. I go to Mayflower Academy. The papers call my school Superchav Academy but it ain't that bad really. It's three years since Clinton Brunton Fletcher stole Miss Brett's Renault Clio and burned it out on the hockey pitch, and to be honest no one in Year Eleven got pregnant last term at all. It's time people built a bridge, got over it, and stopped stereotyping us in such a prejudicial manner.

Our family feud is proper complex. Basically, I want to stay on in Mayflower Sixth Form and get some some exams and get a good job. A job where I can wear lipgloss and not look like a munter and I don't have to pull mashed rats' feet out of lamb kofta all day and go home smelling of a dead sheep's bumhole. My mum, Diane Wood, will kick off big style when I tell her 'cos she says that doing A-Levels is for scroungers, lazing about spending her tax-payer's money studying degrees in nothing to avoid real work. Mum said this to my big sister, Cava-Sue, about seven hundred and forty-nine times and now Cava-Sue has run off to London and is living with a girl called Pixie with blue hair who looks like a homeless too.

Cava-Sue hates my mother and my mother hates Cava-Sue, well, so they pretend but they don't really. They ain't keeping it real at all. Truth to tell, my mum is proper depressed about it all and cries every night and Cava-Sue misses home and is so skint she's been singing on the

London Underground for money. This is well worrying 'cos I have heard Cava-Sue singing and it sounds like someone with their goolies trapped in a revolving door. I am worried she will starve. I wish Cava-Sue would come home 'cos I miss her so much. That's two problems for Kirsten-who-is-trained to be going on with.

The only person who speaks to Cava-Sue regular like is my nan from Chadwell Heath. Nan is trying not to get involved in this 'cos Nan and my mum don't get on. Nan is my dad's mother. Nan jars Mum's head by coming over to our house on Sundays and making gravy without lumps and going through our fridge looking at sell-by dates and making us watch *Last of the Summer Wine* repeats and then falling asleep sitting on the remote control with her teeth out, snoring.

Mum says that Nan has never liked her anyhow 'cos back in 1985 Dad used to have a girlfriend called Flo who had a typing qualification, a green bike with a shopping basket and mousey-brown hair in a side-parting who went to church, and Nan never ever got over the fact that Dad dumped Flo for Mum, 'cos Mum used to wear a tube skirt and a tight jumper and they used to go to see bands in Romford called stuff like Level 42 and come home drunk on brandy.

I just want my family to all get along.

There is no one else for me to talk to about all of this. My brother, Murphy, and dad, Brian, are neither use nor bloody ornament, as Nan would say. They spend all night in the living-room chatting rubbish about West Ham Football Club transfer rumours and then whenever I mention Cava-Sue running away from home it's like they've gone deaf.

I get more sensible conversation from our Staffy, Penny, and believe me she'll be dead soon as the entire street is in a conspiracy to feed her until she is as big as a small horse, and despite being on a strict low-fat/low-sugar diet I found her at number thirty-four just yesterday in Mrs Khan's kitchenette guzzling lamb passanda with a keema nan. She was blowing off garlic and coriander farts all night. Does Kirsten-who-is-trained know anything about dogs?

To make matters worse, me and my best mate, Carrie Draper, have fallen out big time. Carrie has been my best friend in the whole world since Year Seven but then she met this rapper called Bezzie who was a right clown and she turned into a right drippy tart about him. Well, I said some stuff I maybe shouldn't, like that he was a munter and had no skills as an emcee, and now even though Carrie's split up with Bezzie 'cos he says she's a dirty skank, Carrie's still not talking to me, just 'cos I was the one who gave her all her stuff back, when Bezzie wanted to chuck it over her garden wall.

You can't do right for doing wrong in this world can you?

Can someone from *Fast-Track Family Feud* help me make friends again with Carrie 'cos if I got that sorted out then maybe I could do the A-Levels/Cava-Sue/Nan/Mum/Dog's obesity problems on my own?

Thank you for reading my letter. We are all available to appear on *Fast-Track Family Feud* on ITV2 whenever you would like and look forward to hearing from you as soon as possible.

Yours sincerely

Shiraz Bailey Wood.

I printed this out and posted it today. On reflection, maybe I shouldn't have said that we were all available to go on telly, but I got a little bit carried away.

## FRIDAY 3RD OCTOBER

It is my sixteenth birthday today. I didn't tell anyone at school 'cos they'd all want to know what I was doing and the answer is nothing. Mum asked if I wanted to go to the Wimpy for a knickerbockerglory or something. I said no 'cos a) the Wimpy closed down in 2001 and b) I'm not four. Mum said I should stop with the lip or I wouldn't be getting my present, so I shut up quick. Dunno know why I bothered 'cos it was a fluffy hot-water bottle. A bloody fluffy hot-water bottle?! Having paid a bit of attention in Geography recently the last thing I'm going to need with global warming is a hot-water bottle. Mum doesn't give a crap about global warming, she says it'll be nice to get a bit of sun without having to mix with foreigners and eat their food.

If the ice caps do melt and polar bears begin swimming further afield for sustenance I hope they find her betting shop.

Nan came round and gave me a £5 WH Smith's book token and a Terry's Chocolate Orange. No card from Cava-Sue.

## MONDAY 6TH OCTOBER

Carrie and Uma were caught shoplifting in Superdrug in Ilford Mall this afternoon! They got taken down Ilford police station and cautioned. Kezia said that Carrie had two cans of Ambre Solaire spray-tan up her jumper and Uma had a box of condoms and some blue Bourjois eyeshadow down the front of her jeans. Barney Draper had to go and pick Carrie up, then he rang my mum to see if I'd been there with them too. 'No Barney,' said my mother with a face as smug as smug. 'My daughter was in school. In fact she's here now doing her homework.'

My mum put the phone down and cackled like a drain. 'See what I told you?' she said. 'Carrie Draper, shoplifting in Superdrug! They ruined that girl. Ruined her.'

Carrie isn't ruined. But she will be if she carries on hanging out with Uma Brunton-Fletcher.

Sometimes I see Carrie looking over at me when I'm having a laugh in class with Sean and Kezia and everyone, like she wants to join in and all that. I just blank her though 'cos I'm not getting shouted at again.

## THURSDAY 9TH OCTOBER

Still no word back from *Fast-Track Family Feud*. I'm well disappointed. I thought we'd be right up their street. I should never have mentioned about Penny blowing off. The TV producers would have found out for themselves soon enough when she let one rip and the skin on their faces started melting. I've stopped her sleeping in my bed recently 'cos the smell is so bad it can actually wake you up. If you think about that, that's quite impressive.

## FRIDAY 10TH OCTOBER

A birthday card from Cava-Sue arrived today. Four days late but better than nothing. The message said, *For my favourite little sister from Cava-Sue (and Lewis too!)*. It was one of Lewis's homemade efforts. Black cardboard, words and pictures cut out of magazines then glued on to card, with wonky scribbling on it.

Cava-Sue used to say that Lewis's art is full of hidden meaning and one day he'll be a famous artist and we'll sell these cards and make a fortune.

I looked at the card for ages and tried to find some hidden meaning, but the only one I could come up with was he probably wants his head looked at.

There was no message about her coming home.

## SATURDAY IITH OCTOBER

Went to Ilford Mall with my mother today 'cos she wanted to look at a new washing machine 'cos the old one is knackered. We walked through the town centre and my mum was rabbiting on and on about me getting a job and earning some money 'cos then I can help her out buying things like washing machines 'cos after all it'll be me that's using it too. I felt like saying, 'Yeah unless I run away from home like Cava-Sue did,' but I didn't. Me and Mum get along just fine as long as we don't talk about important things. We wandered through the mall and then my mum's face lit up like someone had flipped a switch on her head 'cos she saw Collette Brown outside Cheeky's. Colette's face seemed to be a bit green.

''Ere Collette, how are you love?' my mum said.

'Oh all right, Mrs Wood. Not so bad,' said Collette. 'Just getting some fresh air.'

'Ooh, you been out on the town last night, have you?' smiled my mum.

'Erm . . . Not really,' said Collette. 'I'm, erm, well . . . I'm three months pregnant, actually.'

'Oh!' my mum gasped, really searching about for words. 'Ooooh . . . erm, congratulations, lovey! Good for you!'

'Ta very much,' said Collette, quietly.

'And it's you and your fella Curt—' began my mum.

'Earl!' said Collette, quickly. 'It's my boyfriend Earl's. Earl who owns Cheeky's.'

'Yes, Earl,' said Mum. 'That's right.'

I tried to imagine Collette Brown with a baby. Collette pushing a pram. Collette changing a nappy with her acrylic nail extensions. Collette sitting in every night covered in poo with her tiara on. I couldn't quite picture it.

('You don't have to get knocked up aged twenty by some random, Shiraz!' that's what Cava-Sue said.)

'So was it a surprise?' smiled my mum.

'Well, yeah,' said Collette. 'But y'know we would have probably wanted kids soon enough anyway. Earl loves children.'

'Good for you both,' said my mum. Collette smiled a nervous smile. Then she retched a bit.

'Well, we'll see you again soon, eh? You take it easy,' said my mum as we walked off.

My mum thought for a bit then she said to me, 'See, she's not daft that one? Knocked up by the owner of Cheeky's? She'll be quids in there with him. She'll want for nothing.'

'I think she's quite young to have a baby,' I said.

'She's twenty years old,' said my mum. 'I'm glad I had mine early, got 'em out of the way. There's nothing worse than an old mum. So narrow-minded.'

201

We got the bus home and I went straight into my room and started learning some French vocabulary for my test on Monday. I've heard a language GCSE can be dead useful for getting a good job.

## TUESDAY 21ST OCTOBER

FAST-TRACK FAMILY FEUD
JETSTAR TELEVISION
ROOM 345 ORION HOUSE
LONDON WC3 H78

Dear Shiraz Bailey Wood

Thank you very much for getting in touch with *Fast-Track Family Feud*! We really enjoyed hearing all about your dilemma involving your mum, your nan, your sister Cava-Sue, your brother Murphy, your dad, and not forgetting your famous flatulent dog!

The team at *Fast-Track Family Feud* really feel that we could help you with your problems. Here at *Fast-Track Family Feud*, we give you the chance to air your grievances in public and speak to a trained counsellor.

Please could you give our researchers, Jocasta and Samantha, a call on 0800 435 7880 (we'll call you right back) and we can get the ball rolling.

Yours sincerely

Zac Flinty-Farnham (Producer)

# NOVEMBER

## WEDNESDAY 12TH NOVEMBER

The Wood family appeared on national telly today! No, I can't hardly believe it either but it is TOTALLY TRUE. Go look on YouTube if you think I'm a faker. Luther uploaded it right away and it's had about two thousand seven hundred views already. I am a bloody TV star! The whole thing is totally off the scale. I can hardly explain it. I suppose I should start at the beginning. First thing was that I got a letter back from the *Fast-Track Family Feud* people. That was a shock enough 'cos I'd been watching the show all week and they'd had this one family on last Tuesday called the Barret-Coopers from Doncaster who'd blown up their uncle's house with a pipe bomb over a row about lottery scratch cards, so I was beginning to think that maybe our family feud wasn't that exciting after all.

So the letter arrived and I was proper BUZZING. I rang this woman called Jocasta who sounded quite posh and she rang me straight back to save my bill and she said, 'So are your family still having problems, Shiraz?'

So I said 'Well, Jocasta, my mum is chugging her way through forty Kensitas Club a day and cries when you mention Cava-Sue and last thing I heard about Cava-Sue was that she was wrapping herself into a bacofoil representation of a Victorian chimney sweep and standing very still on a box near the Houses of Parliament to entertain tourists, so you could say that, yeah.'

Jocasta laughed out proper loud then, before she realized I wasn't kidding.

'And what about your nan? Has she been any help?' asked Jocasta.

'Well,' I sighed, 'Nan was over on Sunday, but she had a right go at Mum about not trying to sort things with Cava-Sue. So Mum told her to go and shove her advice somewhere very rude indeed, then Nan shouted "You've no heart, you Di! Just a swinging brick on a rope!" Then Nan left without even eating her Sara Lee chocolate gateau, threatening to move to Benidorm and get the hell out of it, which made me right upset, although Murphy was quite pleased as he got Nan's cake.'

Then Jocasta asked me about our fat dog and I said that no one wanted to take Penny out for a stroll no more on account of the abuse we receive from passers-by in cars about animal cruelty, which I don't really agree with 'cos if you'd seen how happy that dog is when she's eating Jammy Dodgers you'd not think it was cruel at all. Jocasta asked me a load more questions about the family and I rambled on for a bit, then she said she'd put in 'a provisional date' of Wednesday November twelfth. Jocasta said if I gave her some contact details for my family members and connected parties then we 'could get this show on the road'.

I went downstairs and my mum was sitting in front of the telly watching *Britain's Nightmare Plumbers* in her cardigan which used to be white but is now nicotine-coloured. I sat beside her on the couch and she put her arm around my shoulder and played with my hair like she used to do when I was a little girl. I got the letter from *Fast-Track Family Feud* out of my pocket and said, "Ere, Mum, don't flip out or nothing but I wrote to these people the other day.'

I thought she would hit the roof and start jarring me head but she didn't. She just read the letter quietly and sighed and said, 'Well that Kirsten-who-is-trained woman who sits backstage seems like she knows what she's doing, don't she? Maybe we should give it a go.' And before I knew it we were all going on national telly to discuss our problems. Me, Mum, Dad, Murphy, Nan, Cava-Sue and even the dog.

*Fast-Track Family Feud* is filmed in Norwich and the TV people promised to pay for us all to go there and to stay in a hotel overnight and said we'd get our makeup done and said we'd be treated like proper celebrities. I was well excited even though I was dreading the train journey to Norwich 'cos one hour fifty minutes is a long time to be stuck on a train with Mum, Dad, Nan, Murphy and Penny, especially as Nan and Mum would only talk via me like I was an interpreter, plus our dog spent the first half hour out of Liverpool Street Station either washing her own bum or hell-bent on getting to the buffet car 'cos she could smell bacon sandwiches.

'Ask your nan if she wants a cup of tea,' said my mum.

'Mum says do you want a cup of tea, Nan?' I'd say.

'No I'm fine thanks, tell your mother.'

'Nan says she's fine thanks, Mum,' I'd say. Then they both sat with their arms crossed staring out of the window, while Murphy and Dad read the sports section of the *Sun* and pretended everything was fine.

We got picked up at the station by a bloke holding a sign which said *Shiraz Bailey Wood* and put into a swanky people-carrier and taken to our hotel, which was called The Norwich Traveller's Rest and was on a roundabout overlooking a traffic jam. When we got to the front desk the receptionist gave us a form which reminded us that any bills or damages we ran up in the hotel were our responsibility and not *Fast-Track Family Feud*'s and we had to sign a form saying we'd behave ourselves. 'What a flaming liberty! Who do they think we are?' said my mum, but then I reminded her about the Barret-Coopers from Doncaster last week and their pyromaniac son, then Mum admitted the form was probaby a good idea. I hoped we might see Cava-Sue at the hotel but she wasn't there. I started to worry then that she might not come at all.

Soon Jocasta and her friend Samantha arrived to escort us to the TV studio. Jocasta took me off by myself and said she loved my pink tracksuit and gold hoops and said I would be the main focus of our show as I am 'such a spirited, interesting character' which is the sort of thing teachers used to write in my report card when they meant 'gobby annoying cow' but somehow Jocasta made it sound like a good thing.

'OK,' I said, 'but I want my makeup done 'cos I don't want to go on national telly looking butterz.' Then Jocasta laughed and said she'd sort it out.

I sat in the makeup chair and this woman with a spiral perm stuck peach blusher and brown mascara on me like I was thirty or something, then she looked at my hair, which was in a neon-pink scrunchy, and said, 'What do we want done with this then?'

So I said, 'I want it left like that but with more hairspray.'

And the woman said, 'But it's all poking up like a pineapple!'

So I said, 'Have you looked in the mirror recently? Your hair is all frizzy like pubes.'

Then Jocasta nearly spat tea everywhere and the makeup woman shut up after that.

Then Reuben Smart, who is the host of *Fast-Track Family Feud*, came in the room and he shook my hand and said, 'Shiraz Bailey Wood?' and I didn't recognize him at first 'cos in real life he is well scrawny and really brown, like a skeleton dipped in Marmite. Then Reuben said, 'Are you the girl who has all of Westlife's faces tattooed on your back?'

And Jocasta said, 'No Reuben, Shiraz is the girl with

the runaway sister and the morbidly obese dog.'

'Ah, OK, right,' said Reuben. 'Well, Shiraz, you have a good show. And remember, plenty of energy. Plenty of backchat. No swearing because it's live television. We're all your friends here so let's get all the tension out in the open and work through it.'

'Is my sister, Cava-Sue, here?' I said.

'She's just arrived, she's talking to Kirsten at the moment,' said Jocasta.

They stuck a microphone up my top and clipped it on to my bra, then told me not to go for a wee or anything 'cos everyone upstairs in the control room can hear the woosh sound and they put them all on a tape and laugh at it at the Christmas party. Then they said, 'Five minutes to go, we're going to take you through to the studio now, Shiraz,' and they took me through on to 'the floor' and placed me on a seat in front of about a hundred people who looked a lot like the Brunton-Fletcher family 'cos a lot of them had funny teeth and looked quite aggressive. When I looked closer at the front row, I saw Pixie, Lewis, my dad and my brother. They didn't look very happy to be there. Not one little bit.

'And counting down . . . five-four-three-two-one,' said a bloke in a headset. 'Going live!'

All of a sudden the really cheesy *Fast-Track Family Feud* theme music began to play and we were on LIVE NATIONAL TELEVISION and Reuben made his face look very very serious.

'Good afternoon and welcome to another edition of *Fast-Track Family Feud*!' said Reuben. 'Now, we've got a case today that I know is going to shock you to the core, just as it shocked me and all of our researchers!'

All the crowd sat forward in their seats looking proper excited.

'Shiraz!' said Reuben, suddenly turning to me. 'Thanks for coming. Tell me about your mother Diane . . . She's a total nightmare isn't she?'

'What?' I said, feeling a bit shocked. 'Well. No. I wouldn't say that.'

'Well you said it to our researchers,' said Reuben. 'You said your mum drove your own sister out of the house. You said she smokes like a chimney! And she drinks too, doesn't she? Didn't you tell them that your mum once drank so much Peach Lambrella that she was dancing about the house making a right old carry on . . . and she got you drunk too!'

The crowd all began grumbling. This sounded really bad. I looked up at the monitor and there was a subtitle on the bottom of the screen that read: *Mum! Leave us alone – you're wrecking our home!*

''Ere, hang on a minute!' I laughed. 'What I said was my mum and me had a drink on New Year's Eve.'

Reuben ruffled his notes and gave me a black look.

'A drink is a drink whatever date it says on the calendar, Shiraz,' he said.

The crowd gave him a round of applause. I looked at

my dad and he was looking proper angry now.

'My mum's not a drinker. And she only smokes because she's stressed!' I said loudly. 'And she's stressed because our sister Cava-Sue has ran off to London.'

'Ah . . . Cava-Sue?' said Reuben, looking at his notes. 'Is this the one who is working as a stripper?'

The crowd mumbled excitedly again. A man in a beanie hat cheered. Murphy looked really unhappy. Suddenly someone began shouting in the audience. It was Pixie.

'Cava-Sue Wood is not a stripper, you bloody liar,' she yelled at Reuben. 'She is a mime artist and a singer! She does NOT strip. I'm her friend so I should know!'

The crowd were loving this.

'Wooooo! Another stripper!' shouted some blokes on the back row. 'Strip! Strip! Strip! Strip!'

'I never said any of this!' I said loudly, although no one was listening by now. 'My mum isn't a drunk and my sister isn't a stripper.'

'Sorry, Shiraz, could you speak louder?' shouted Reuben.

'They're both proper nice people really!' I shouted. 'They just don't get on 'cos Cava-Sue wants to do her own thing and Mum keeps getting on her case all the time. So Cava-Sue has gone. I just want everyone in my family to be friends again.'

The audience clapped then like I'd said something right.

'Well let's bring out Cava-Sue and see what she has to say about all this!' said Reuben.

Suddenly the glittery doors at the side of the stage flung open and there was our Cava-Sue, standing there in her white fluffy fur coat, a smock dress, footless tights and high heels. She looked FURIOUS. She stormed towards me and began wagging her finger.

'Shiraz, you are a liberty!' she said. 'What did you go and tell them I was a druggy and a stripper for? That ain't true!'

'Woo-hoo! Fight!' roared the crowd.

'I didn't tell them that at all!' I shouted above the noise.

Suddenly I was beginning to realize why *Fast-Track Family Feud* is always worth setting Sky+ for.

'Take a seat, Cava-Sue,' said Reuben. 'Now there's no use shouting and screaming. Just be calm and make your point.'

'I'm not a stripper,' said Cava-Sue, crossly. 'I ran away from home as I am protesting against the outdated, unjust ideology that is bandied around our home as common law by my mother!' Cava-Sue took a deep breath and carried on, 'I am a post feminist, green voter and a free spirit! I'll wear whatever I want and go wherever I want. No one can tell me what to do!'

Cava-Sue sat back in her chair looking triumphant. Everyone in the audience stared at her like she'd just announced that she was a giant hot-dog from the planet

Tharg. Well, everyone except Pixie, who clapped dead loudly.

'Woo-hoo! You go, Cav!' shouted Pixie.

My dad, my brother and Lewis all covered their faces with their hands.

'So where are you living now, Cava-Sue?' asked Reuben. 'On the streets? That's a fine way to live your life, isn't it?'

'No, not on the streets . . . mmmm . . . in my friend's flat,' mumbled Cava-Sue.

'Oh really?' said Reuben. 'But you told our researchers you were going to be homeless by December as you couldn't afford rent.'

Cava-Sue winced a bit.

'Mmmm . . . well . . . yeah . . . but I'll work something out,' she said huffily.

'Homeless? For Christmas?' said Reuben. 'Seems like a high price to pay to get one over on your mum. Even if she is an alcoholic who mistreats your dog!'

The audience gasped again.

'Shame on all of you!' yelled a man on the second row with yellow teeth and a spider's web facial tattoo.

'Well, that's not strictly true,' tutted Cava-Sue.

'Let's be honest here! The facts speak for themselves, Cava-Sue,' said Reuben. 'The sooner we all face the facts the sooner we can build some bridges!'

Everyone cheered at that.

'Now,' said Reuben, before anyone else could speak.

'We've got someone else backstage with an opinion on your family! Bring on Nan and bring on Penny the dog!'

Oh my days, I thought, beginning to feel very worried. What a mess.

Everyone clapped as the glittery doors opened and out came Nan, who appeared to have the same blusher and mascara on as me and her hair sprayed in a weird bouffant. Nan was dragging along our dog, who had obviously been bribed with something chocolaty to behave. Nan sat down on her chair and threw Reuben one of her hackiest Nan looks.

'Y'know, YOU young man,' she grumped, 'you're the reason I'm not renewing my TV licence! You're supposed to be helping this family, not stirring things up.'

I looked into the monitor and I could see a shot of my mum backstage with Kirsten-who-is-trained holding her hand. She looked like she was crying.

'Exactly, Nan!' shouted Cava-Sue. 'This is exploitation of the working man by the chattering classes in its basest form! It's disgusting!'

'I agree!' I said, pretending to know what she meant.

'Well, Nan, what have you got to say about Diane Wood?' said Reuben, ignoring them.

'I say let Diane speak for herself,' shouted my nan. 'All these accusations are blown out of proportion! Di doesn't mistreat the dog! She loves that dog.'

'This dog is morbidly obese!' said Reuben, pompously.

Nan narrowed her eyes at Reuben.

'Well we don't all have to run around in the shower to get wet like you, you bloody miserable bag of bones!' huffed Nan. 'You look like a whippet on its back legs! You could do with a nice pork chop!'

Everyone laughed then, except Reuben.

'It's understandable that you want to lash out at someone,' said Reuben to Nan patronizingly, then he put his hand to his earpiece. 'Y'know, I don't think we're getting any sense from these people. I think we should meet the woman who is responsible for these out-of-control kids and that dog! Bring out Diane Wood!'

The *Fast-Track Family Feud* theme tune began to play and in the monitor we could see my mother refusing to go out on stage, then being literally dragged by the arm by Kirsten-who-is-trained and pushed through the glittery doors. The crowd saw her and began to boo and hiss!

'Boooooo! Shame on you!' hissed one woman in a blue anorak and ski pants. Me, Cava-Sue and Nan looked at each other in horror. I know that right at that moment all the Wood women felt EXACTLY the same as me. Really annoyed. I mean, it's all right for us to slag each other off, but if anyone else slags the Wood family, that is TOTALLY NOT ON. We all had to stick together.

'Booooooo!' hissed ski-pant woman.

'Oh shut your faces!' shouted Cava-Sue.

'You don't even know us!' I yelled.

'You're like a bleeding lynch-mob!' said Nan.

Mum walked over to her seat and sat down beside

Cava-Sue, and they both looked at each other proper nervous.

'So Diane,' said Reuben. 'This is a right fine mess you've created here, isn't it?'

My mum just shook her head and sniffed a bit.

'Is there anything you want to say?' said Reuben.

'Not really,' said my mum. 'I'm a bit upset.'

'Oh come on,' said Reuben. 'Don't miss your chance.'

'Well OK,' said my mum. 'I just want to say that I know I'm not perfect. And I know I'm a bit of a nightmare. But I've always worked my hardest for these kids. I'm not Wonderwoman.'

Me and Cava-Sue looked at her guiltily then.

'And god knows I've made mistakes. And maybe I ain't good at apologizing. But I always loved the very bones of these kids. Loved 'em!'

It felt funny 'cos my mum never ever says she loves us. But when she said it, we both weren't surprised or nothing. Deep down we both knew she loved us more than life itself. I reckon people don't have to make a big song and dance about loving you for you to know that you're loved. They don't in my family anyhow.

'So what do you want then, Diane?' said Reuben.

'Well I know I don't want my Cava-Sue to be homeless,' said my mum. 'I want her to come home. I want her to know that I'm sorry.'

'I'm sorry too, Mum,' said Cava-Sue.

I couldn't believe what I was hearing.

'Say it to Cava-Sue, not to me!' shouted Reuben.

My mother turned to Cava-Sue.

'Just get yerself home, love,' said my mum in a quiet voice. 'I won't go on about you being a scrounger or nothing no more. And we'll forget the housework chart. Let's start again?'

Cava-Sue looked at my mum for a few seconds, then she put out her hand and put it over my mum's on the chair arm. Cava-Sue didn't say anything, but we all knew from that moment that she was coming home.

I'd only went and done it! She who dares wins!

Everyone cheered, even the woman in the ski pants who'd been told off for swearing at Mum ten minutes previously.

'Isn't that great to see, ladies and gentlemen?' said Reuben. 'Another *Fast-Track Family Feud* solved! We're good at this, aren't we? That just about wraps up this section, we've just got a few of your phonecalls to take. Line one? Philip in Birmingham?'

'Er, hello Reuben!' said the voice on the line. 'Yeah, where will Cava-Sue be stripping next?'

'I'm not a stripper, you sexist oaf!' sighed Cava-Sue.

'Moving on? Er, next call. Line two,' said Reuben. 'Megan in Cleetermoor?'

'Hello?' said the woman. 'This is the best family feud I've seen for ages. You lot are so funny! You're funnier than that family from Wigan who cut their sister's hair with a hedge trimmer! Brilliant!'

'Thank you Megan . . . Now line three, Carrie from Goodmayes?' said Reuben. 'Carrie, are you there? Carrie?!'

My heart almost stopped. Nah, it couldn't be.

'Er, all right,' said the girl's voice. 'I . . . erm, well . . . I just had a message for Shiraz Bailey Wood. It's Carrie Draper here. I just wanted to say, Shiz, that I'm dead proud of you. You're a proper star. And I'm sorry, right? And we'll sort it out, right . . .'

My heart nearly burst through my chest with happiness.

'We're out of time,' said Reuben. 'I'll have to say good—'

'And I just wanted to say . . . 'ere, Shiz, you see that bloke on the front row with the tattoo on his face?'

'Er yeah?' I said.

'That's your boyfriend that is!' shouted Carrie. 'See you back in Goodmayes, Shizza. Superchav Academy for ever!'

I laughed so much that I hardly heard Reuben wrapping the show up 'cos there was no more time. The Wood family all fell out of the studio in a really excellent mood. In fact, backstage Kirsten-who-is-trained didn't need to give us no more counselling or anything, she said we were just fine as we were.

And that's what happened on *Fast-Track Family Feud*. As I say, if you don't believe me go on YouTube and look for yourself. I ain't no faker.

# DECEMBER

## MONDAY IST DECEMBER

One of the best things about being proper famous, like me and Tabitha Tennant from *Big Brother* are, is how just popping to the shops for a pint of milk and a scratchcard can be so much fun. 'Shiraz Bailey Wooooood!' folk yell at me in the street in Goodmayes. '*Fast-Track Family Feuuuuuuuud!*' Some kids even film me on their phones! I even signed an autograph in the chicken section of Iceland. Carrie thinks it is all well jokes. It's been two weeks since my TV appearance and me and Carrie have already been plotting ways to 'increase our profile'. We're thinking of auditioning for *X-Factor* as a duo singing the Mariah Carey song 'Hero'. Carrie can do all the high notes. I can do all the low notes. We're going to call ourselves Half Rice/Half Chips.

I'm so glad that me and Carrie are best mates again. We have promised to never ever let stupid boys come between us again. Carrie is TOTALLY over Bezzie now. She says she don't care about him at all. He sent her a text last week asking if they could have a chat soon so he could 'get some closure'. She was all 'I'm not bothered, mate. See ya later. Plenty more fish in the sea'.

It's like having old Carrie back again.

I don't think about Wesley Barrington Bains II in that mushy way no more. He's just a mate. I mean, when I heard this week that Wesley and Dee-Dee had split up it's not like I got my hopes up or anything. I'm keeping it real.

## WEDNESDAY 3RD DECEMBER

I am proper excited about Christmas this year! Cava-Sue and my dad went to B&Q today and bought some new decorations for the front of the house. Mum says we should push the boat out and celebrate the Wood family being back together again. They came back with a three-metre-high multi-coloured Santa light display. Lewis and Dad are nailing it to the front of the house right now. Cava-Sue says she feels a bit guilty 'cos it's going to waste loads of electricity, but she couldn't resist it. Cava-Sue says it's Christmas so she's going to worry about her carbon footprint later. I love having her home.

## FRIDAY 5TH DECEMBER

Carrie is trying a lot harder at school like me now too. We want to stay on in sixth form if our GCSEs go OK. I still haven't told my mum.

Me and Carrie ain't swots or nothing. It's just that if Half Rice/Half Chips don't take off we're definitely going to need a back-up career. I think we'll be OK though. When Carrie does her bit of 'Hero' and she shuts her eyes and waves her arms about she looks like a proper diva. We did it in the lunch hall today and almost everyone said we were brilliant, aside from Uma Brunton-Fletcher and Latoya Bell, who said we're a pair of right silly cows.

## SUNDAY 7TH DECEMBER

The Wood Christmas decorations have been officially switched on! They are well good!! First Aunty Glo popped over with her niece to have a look, then Mrs Khan came too. Then cars began to stop outside the house and take photos. Then at about 7pm I went to the front door and there was £2.78 in loose change on the front door mat! People must reckon that we're collecting for charity! Murphy tried to pocket it but Cava-Sue gave him a Chinese burn and took it back. Cava-Sue has made a sign for the front window saying that the Wood family are saving up to buy an alpaca for a Peruvian mountain farmer. I have looked up what an alpaca is on the Internet and it is like a furry buck-toothed goat/sheep thingy. If it comes here first it's sleeping with Cava-Sue in the top bunk. But I don't reckon it will be much good with ladders.

## MONDAY 8TH DECEMBER

Wesley Barrington Bains II knocked on our door this evening. I was sort of shocked and embarrassed all at once as I was writing my Christmas cards, wearing baggy pyjama bottoms and my dad's old cardigan and no makeup or hoops or nothing.

'Y'all right?' I said, coming to the front door.

'Yeah, not bad innit?' he said.

We looked at each other for a while.

'You split up with Dee-Dee?' I said, like I wasn't bothered or nothing, just making conversation.

'Yeah, man, it weren't working out,' he said. 'We wanted different stuff and that, innit?'

I folded my arms and leaned against the door frame.

'Like what different stuff?' I said. The giant multi-coloured Santa was flashing on and off, illuminating both of our faces.

'Well, like . . . she wanted me to go round her house and that, like, all the time and hang out,' said Wesley. 'And I didn't want that, innit.'

'Right,' I said. There was a long silence.

'So what you doin' round here?' I said.

'Oh I was just passing,' he said. 'And, erm, I wanted to give you some, erm, money for them alampakara wotsits you're collecting for. It's a good cause, innit.' Wesley put his hand in his trackie bottoms and brought out £3.

'Cheers,' I said, taking the money and sticking it my pocket. There was a longer silence.

'Well I better be getting off then,' Wesley said. 'I'm meeting Bezzie. We're going to start laying down some tracks.'

'Right, see ya then,' I said.

Wesley wandered down the path.

''Ere, Wesley,' I said. 'Do you even know what an alpaca is?'

Wesley turned around. He thought for a bit.

'It's a big rabbit, innit?' he said.

I smiled to myself.

'It's a bit like that,' I said, nodding my head slowly.

Then I was very brave. ''Ere, Wesley,' I said. 'Did you come round here for that or for something else?'

Wesley looked a bit embarrassed.

'Well, yeah,' he said. 'I wondered, like, if you wanted to come out with me next week or something? Get a pizza or something, innit?'

'Er . . . yeah,' I said, trying not to smile too much like a proper loon. 'Yeah! Yeah, I would.'

'Oh, oh right,' he said, looking well relieved. 'That's sweet then, innit. I'll send you a text or something. Sort something out.' Then he jumped in his car and disappeared into the night, leaving me standing under an illuminated Santa's sleigh with a big smile on my gob like I'd just had a lucky scratchcard.

I still can't believe it happened.

## THURSDAY 11TH DECEMBER

Ms Bracket has made me, Carrie and Luther 'student liaison contacts' for the Mayflower Academy 2007 Winter Festival! Basically, this means that we're helping sort out the Christmas Carol Service on the nineteenth, except this year there will CERTAINLY be no carols and no religious stuff at all 'cos of last year's 'fiasco' with the rude carols and Sonia Cathcart's dad kicking off and all that palaver.

Mr Bamblebury says that we should try to make it 'a celebration of light', 'cos then it will be a little bit like Jewish Hannukah and a little bit like Eid, and a little bit like a Pagan celebration, and we can all get together and sing some songs from the *Come and Praise* songbook about robins and have a plastic beaker of non-alcoholic mulled wine and THAT CAN'T OFFEND ANYONE CAN IT?!

Mr Bamblebury looks like he needs a holiday.

No word at all from Wesley. Did I imagine all that?

## MONDAY 15TH DECEMBER

Wesley Barrington Bains II texted me tonight! He is taking me for a pizza on Friday night as soon as he gets paid from Argos. IT'S LIKE A PROPER DATE!!!

I've never been on a date before. I can't imagine sitting eating a whole pizza in front of him. What if I get it all over my face? And what will we talk about? And what will I wear? As if I ain't got enough to think about. I've got a Winter Festival to organize. Me, Carrie, Kezia and Luther spent all lunch hour making five hundred metres of festive paper chains out of old recycling paper to decorate the hall. It's quite pretty if you squint. I hope it all goes OK.

## WEDNESDAY 18TH DECEMBER

Oh my days.

## THURSDAY 19TH DECEMBER

There is no way that I can POSSIBLY be to blame for what happened at the Mayflower Academy 2007 Winter Festival. NO WAY. I wasn't anywhere near it. ON MY LIFE. All I can say, right, is that if the police want to come and take this diary as evidence they totally can 'cos then they'll see that I was proper innocent and who they want to be looking at is Uma Brunton-Fletcher 'cos she was the one messing about.

So we're all in the school hall, right, all of Year Nine, Ten and Eleven, all the mums and dads and the teachers, and we've sang the song about the robin, and Sean Burton has been on and done his 'Poem for Peace', and then some kids dressed as snowdrops have done their 'representation of winter via the power of dance' and everything's going well and no one's got punched and we're all happy. Then all that has to happen is Elliot Marsden from Year Nine has to walk through the crowd with a candle on a plate singing 'The Greatest Love Of All' by Whitney Houston, 'cos there's a line in it about 'children being the future' which is sort of true if you think about it, except by the time he got halfway through the crowd, he let out a scream that was most definitely not in the song.

It turned out that as he passed the Year Eleven seats, Uma Brunton-Fletcher has got some hairspray out of her handbag and given his candle a quick squirt. Now in fairness, I reckon all Uma wanted to do was give him a shock and make Latoya laugh, but what happened was the flame shot right out and caught hold of one of the paper chains hanging off the tree, which set fire to another chain, then another, then another, 'cos we'd made like five hundred metres of them.

Then everyone began to scream, then Ms Bracket shouted, 'Don't panic! Don't panic. Evacuate the assembly hall! Walk slowly!' And of course everyone didn't, they just ran for it, pushing each other and shouting. Then Mr Gilligan got the fire extinguisher and he was squirting the tree like mad but it was still on fire and eventually he gave up and called 999.

Me, Carrie, Luther, Sonia Cathcart, Sean Burton, the Bean twins, Kezia and Chantalle Strong all stood by the school gates and watched as the flames began to take hold of the assembly hall. We waited for the fire engine and we waited and waited but it didn't come, and eventually Mr Bamblebury called 999 again and the fire brigade said they were sorry but they were on their works dinner and they'd assumed it was another Mayflower end-of-term prank so they'd been finishing their Christmas pudding. And by that point the roof of the assembly hall had pretty much gone and the local newspaper and TV crews had arrived, and that's how we ended up on the front of the *Ilford Bugle* with the headline *YET ANOTHER CHRISTMAS SHAMBLES FOR SUPERCHAV ACADEMY.*

This year it was totally not my fault, so in a funny way that is progress.

## FRIDAY 20TH DECEMBER

I went to Pizza Partyland in Romford tonight with Wesley Barrington Bains II. He picked me up in his banana-yellow Golf at 7.30pm. The entire family stood at the window and waved me off, which was totally embarrassing but made Wesley laugh lots. Wesley thinks my family are proper jokes. I s'pose they have their moments. I thought it might be a bit awkward going out on a date with Wesley 'cos we have been just good friends for a long time, but it wasn't at all. We had the Ho Ho Ho – Festive Partyland Special which was a turkey-and-stuffing pizza with jalapenos and Christmas-pudding ice cream to follow. We drove the long way home afterwards and sat outside my house for a bit in the car, talking about life and all that. He gave me a kiss. A proper kiss. Properly on the mouth. His lips are lovely and he closes his eyes when he kisses. I am so happy that I keep wanting to be sick.

He is the most beautiful boy in the whole world ever.

## THURSDAY 25TH DECEMBER – CHRISTMAS DAY

A lot of people moan about Christmas but I don't know why 'cos it is proper amazing. Cava-Sue sat up in bed this morning at about 8am and she laughed and shouted, ''Ere Shiraz, Santa's been! He's been!' And I thought she was maybe still drunk 'cos she was right tipsy when she climbed the ladder last night, but then I sat up in bed and she was right, there were two bags at the end of our bunks with boxes of chocolate and Top Shop gift tokens and some necklaces and gold hoops and stuff! Mum is still swearing down dead it wasn't her.

I went downstairs and Dad was wandering about in a pair of flashing antlers reminding everyone about how early he had to get up for the turkey, and the dog was begging Quality Street and Murphy got a new PS2 game called Death Swamp 3, and Mum was in her nightie having a go at killing swampbeasts. Me and Cava-Sue peeled some spuds and danced to Radio One, and Murphy never took the mickey once about me and Wesley, and Cava-Sue didn't pretend to not know any of the 'commercial songs', and Mum never moaned about Cava-Sue being drunk last night, and we all laughed a lot. That's the good thing about Christmas Day, it's all about getting along.

Nan came over at twelve o'clock and we all had a glass of sparkly wine with orange in it, like rich folk do. Then we ate Christmas dinner and Christmas pudding and no one mentioned the burned chipolatas, and the dog was allowed a plate of turkey and stuffing and we wore wonky paper-hats and we told silly jokes and Dad got a bit drunk and did his Elvis-Presley-on-the-toilet impression again.

Nan and Mum got on quite well and no one called Cava-Sue or Lewis scroungers. Then Wesley Barrington Bains II came round for a Christmas drink and my dad, brother and Lewis whipped him off to the kitchen and they played poker for money and drank lagers.

I've just opened Nan's pressies. She got me another diary. And this big huge massive book which is the *Complete Works of Shakespeare*. Nan says it will come in handy next year when I stay on and study. Cava-Sue and Nan both agree that I'll have to tell Mum soon, 'cos it'll cause World War Three when she finds out. They both say I might as well get it over and done with as soon as possible.

But as I say, Christmas is all about getting along together and peace and goodwill to mankind and that sort of malarkey.

I'll probably tell her tomorrow.

# Can't get enough of Shiraz?
## Then look out for the next of her slammin' diaries

## OH MY DAYS!

I've only gone and passed SEVEN GCSEs! Dad and Cava-Sue are chuffed to bits. Murphy reckons I cheated. Mum is pulling her best dog's bum face. She's not happy, I can tell ...

So, Mayflower Sixth Form here I come! Time to ditch the gold hoops and the spray tan and get myself a long scarf, some A4 folders and a new pencil case. Shiraz Bailey Wood is entering a new phase. Clever, sophisticated and definitely not skiving off ... Staying real ...

http://shirazbaileywood.bebo.com